WYLDBLOOD
MAGAZINE

Issue 5 – October/November 2021

Contents

Wyldblood Magazine #5, October/November 2021 (ISBN: 978-1-914417-04-7). © 2021 Wyldblood and contributors. **Publisher:** Wyldblood Press, Thicket View, Bakers Lane, Maidenhead SL6 6PX UK. www.wyldblood.com **Editor:** Mark Bilsborough. **Fiction editor** Sandra Baker. **First readers:** Vaughan Stanger, Mike Lewis, Rebecca Ruvinsky. **Subscriptions:** 6 issues epub/mobi/pdf delivered to your inbox £15. 6 issue print subscriptions £35. www.wyldblood.com/magazine Single issues available worldwide via Amazon and from Wyldblood:

Submissions: we are regularly open for submissions of flash fiction, short stories and novels – check our website for our current status and requirements. We are a paying market. We also need artwork, people to review us, and people to review *for* us. Email contact@wyldblood.com

Editorial

Welcome to our latest collection of science fiction and fantasy, with stories about ghosts, time travel, the dark side of the Internet, dragons, thought control, the end of the world, exotic clothing and mind over matter, plus a clutch of reviews.

We're into our second year as a publishing company now, which makes it seem less of a rush and more of a reality. As well as the magazine, we've been publishing flash fiction every week on our website www.wyldblood.com and we've got a growing number of novel length titles on our roster, not least our collection of werewolf stories, the *Call of the Wyld*, out now in paperback and as an ebook but shortly to be reissued in hardback, which we're all very excited about.

We're at the point in our publishing journey where initial enthusiasm and that know-nothing feeling that we can conquer the world gives way to tempered realism and cold hard pragmatism. Let's face it, scaling Everest sounds easy after a bottle of wine throwing ideas around a dinner table, but get to Base Camp and the mountain looms high ahead (incidentally we ran an outstanding short story about mountaineering in issue 3 – Denali Stannard's *Fixed Line*, where the ghosts of the fallen haunt the slopes…) So now the challenge is consolidation and expansion. We've yet to publish our first original novel (though we've had many excellent submissions which we're – ahem – taking our time over) but when we do, we want to get it right – and our standards are high, as I'm sure regular readers of this magazine can confirm. Expect a slate of four new novels from us in 2022, plus our Steampunk anthology, *Runs Like Clockwork*, out for Christmas, and a year's best anthology sometime in the new year. We'll also be exploring new distribution channels, expanding our community of reviewers and ARC readers and nudging our tendrils into all sorts of previously unexplored nooks and crannies.

One of the things I'm particularly proud of is that our contributors (and, it seems, our readers) come from all over the place. I gather location data on everyone who sends us a story (one day I'll bore you all with stats and spreadsheets but not today, and not here) and although most of our fiction comes from the US and the UK, we've got stories from Germany, Canada and Sri Lanka in this issue, and we've recently published Flash Fiction from the Lebanon, Sweden and Israel, amongst other places. I love that we're an international community, and I love the different approaches I see from different parts of the world. But we haven't had any stories from Antarctica yet – is there someone on a research station out there with time on their hands trying not to freeze? I hear typing warms the fingers…

We'll be back again in November with another fine collection of stories. Until then, stay safe and happy reading.

Mark

A Stranger, Passing Through
Holly Barratt

I sit by the window hiccupping and I can't even remember a time when I didn't have hiccups. Every time I think the hiccups have stopped, and I'm about to compose myself, get up smooth myself down, brush my hair and head downstairs for breakfast, another hiccup comes and I'm right back where I started. This is my life now, I think, and it's a joke, but I'm still annoyed.

The morning sunlight is shining through the slats of the shutters. Lines of light fall on the floor, onto my lap. I feel the warmth of them cut across my throat and eyes. There's a narrow gap in between the two, and beyond them only the air outside this fourth-floor hotel suite. The shutters are held together with a little metal hook and every so often they clack-clack together in the breeze, a counter-rhythm to my hiccups. My insides jumping up my throat and back down again, unprompted.

Shutters like this are a continental thing. In England we had curtains, thick and dusty, or else with mould creeping up from the bottom. Drawn back from closed windows in pigtails. Windows shut for most of the year, the condensation rising, the rain running down them. Windows shut, doors closed, our lunches indoors, our parties indoors, our narrow city streets lined with buildings made of tight packed brick, rising up to the sky, a roof of stone or a roof of smog. Our bodies laced in with layers of tights, cardigans, coats, scarves, carrying umbrellas and bags of supplies should the weather change. Always so heavy. I always felt so hemmed in in England, enclosed in a box, weighed down by artificial warmth. I longed for travel, and I imagined these other places full of lightness, with endless space stretching out towards the sea or the mountains, to walk around in a t-shirt and bare legs, with no bags, and no contingency plan.

Yet here I am, on the inside of the shutters, viewing Italy in narrow strips of light. I would like to walk holding an umbrella now; I would like the armour of a coat and scarf to guard me against winter and to walk through streets lined with tessellated buildings. I would like to watch rain creep its way down glass and I would like to smell damp, and cold cooked meats and warm stale beer. I would like that very much.

Hiccup.

I thought here I would feel free. When I met Max and he promised to whisk me away. He said he felt hemmed in by England too. Hemmed in by bad memories. Hemmed in by stuffy attitudes, boring office jobs, and petty gossip. He loved the anonymity of travel. He said he never wanted roots. Never wanted to be stuck. Changing and shifting everywhere he went. Always a stranger. I wanted that too. I wanted for us to be strangers together.

Hiccup

But the Mediterranean summer is too hot. Sun imprisons you here like rain does in England. You sit in your air-conditioned room breathing in what you just breathed out. Air cycling through your body again and again. I don't speak the language, and when I try a few halting words, the natives sigh, shake their heads, switch to English to sell me my meal or my bus ticket, complete our business with a fixed smile and a polite "Madame". Then they turn to Max, switch back to Italian, and their faces start to move again. Sometimes the men call out to me "Ciao Bella", "you want to come for a drink?" then they chatter to each other in Italian and I don't know whether I'm a goddess, a whore or a hag to them. Only that I am on the outside. A visitor. Passing through.

"Speak to me in Italian," I said to him "How can I ever learn if no-one will talk to me?"

"We'll not be here forever," he said "There's no point learning Italian, they don't speak it anywhere but Italy. French would be better. Or Spanish even."

"Then teach me French."

"I'm not a good teacher. You can learn when we get there. Take proper lessons."

But now I am in Italy and hemmed in by my Englishness. Max was fluent in three languages. Two different passports. Work he could do from anywhere. How can a man like that be hemmed in by anything? By memories, he says. He's an unlucky man. An unhappy man. I was his happy ever after. The light at the end of his tunnel.

I said "I don't want to be the light at the end of your tunnel. I want to walk with you through the dark."

He said "nothing is dark with you around. I'm happy now. We're happy. We're free."

Hiccup.

I am not drunk. The last drink I had was one that Max brought me, as he did, every day, every evening, sitting at this window with the shutters clacking. Only one drink. A brandy and lemonade. I prefer beer. Beer isn't ladylike and gives you gas. Well, here I am with hiccups anyway.

I don't remember how long I've been here. I remember other things but they seem so distant and small. Sitting on a plane, checking into a hotel, drinking a cappuccino and Max telling me that milky coffee should only be drunk before lunch – all those things seem like childhood memories even though they can't have been a month ago? A week ago? An hour ago? I can't imagine what it's like to not have hiccups. I can't remember what the room looks like behind me.

These lines of light and warmth. They haven't moved. They should have travelled down my body, narrowing as the sun gets higher. Perhaps I haven't been sitting here as long as I imagined. But that click-clack of the shutters: it's the exact same click-clack each time. I watch it, the left shutter moves out slightly, pulls on the hook, the right one follows, then they're pulled back and clack together. Then I hiccup. Then the breeze again, cuts through the warmth, then the left shutter moves, then the right, then they clack, then I hiccup. Then the breeze. And I notice the church bell in the distance – the same flat sound, again and again. It should be striking the quarter hour, the half hour, the next hour – but it doesn't. Everything repeats. It's the same. How long have I been here? The stripe on my brow and across my wrist warming. My thighs close together, my right hand in my lap with my thumb just touching the first finger like that. Hiccupping the same hiccup. Breathing the same breath. Have I even blinked?

And then I decide to move. It's all I need to do. To decide. I move my thumb away from my finger. I straighten my back. I lift a hand to my face. One-two-three.

And I don't hiccup.

And the bells don't ring and click-clack of the shutters changes its rhythm. The stripes of warmth fall down my body to the floor and my face feels cold. My body feels cold, but still. I feel no draft, no breeze, no movement. I see the breeze. Hear the breeze. But I don't feel it on my skin. I twist my body to the bedside table. My hairbrush is not where I left it. My fingers brush the bedside table but feel nothing. There is a novel in French. I feel light as ash. There is a glass with the water from melted ice at the bottom.

I remember the brandy and lemonade. I was standing by the window. Did I put down the glass? There? Anywhere? I was standing by the window. The shutters were open. Banging against the wall. I had hiccups. I always get hiccups, after a drink. After Max's drinks. I was lighter than ash. Then heavy as an asteroid. Falling. I remember falling. I can't handle my drink. I was homesick. I drank too much. I was unlucky. Max was unlucky.

To lose one wife might be considered a misfortune. To lose two?

I pull myself upwards, it feels more like floating than standing. Like in yoga when they say make the body light. I spin. The room behind me is unfamiliar. The shape is the same. My hairbrush is not there. The bedclothes are different. When were those changed? There is make up scattered across the dressing table. Something yellow draped over a chair. I could never wear yellow. It doesn't work with my skin tone. These are another woman's things. I know it before she enters.

She has fashionable blonde hair, a French braid that I never had the patience for, a subtle streak of violet. She wears red lipstick. A deep blue satin blouse, half tucked into loose jeans. It all speaks of relaxed chic, but her eyes are wide, her red lips pressed together, she fiddles with a gold stud earring, twizzling it and twizzling it. She sits down on the chair as Max follows her in. Neither of them see me. I am not really here.

Max is anxious too. His shirt sleeves are rolled up, and there's a wet patch spreading across his chest. I remember the smell of that, sweat when fresh and just cooked by sun. He scrapes a hand through his hair. It's longer now, still shiny and black, with flecks of white just above the ears. I remember it felt like lametta on a Christmas tree, running my hands through it. How can it feel so silky without conditioner? I asked him. I'm so jealous of your hair.

"All women are jealous of my hair," he said, and his hands were on my waist and he was kissing me. And I thought I could smell Italy on his skin. I thought I could smell the world.

"Do you think…" he says to the woman he can see. "I know, I hate asking this."

He walks over and kneels by her side, and his hand is on her waist.

"Perhaps you could ask your father for a loan? Just for the last little bit? I'm good for the rest, you know that – but if Garcia can't pay me until next month we'll miss out. I really want to be able to take you to Guadeloupe."

The woman says something in French. I haven't spoken French since my D-grade GCSE, but I know it when I hear it. Max speaks French back to her. Then they switch to English.

"OK, sure, I can ask. But after I pay him back that's the last of it. I told you Max I really want to sever that connection. I'm never going back."

Her accent isn't French. It might be American. Maybe Canadian. Perhaps even Irish. I don't know. I'm not good with accents, I would have got better, if I travelled more. She raises her hand and runs it through his hair. I can almost feel the silk black strands on the skin of her fingers.

"I can't believe you never use conditioner," she says. "I think you're a liar."

"Never," he says. "Could I ever look into those big blue eyes and tell a lie?"

He touches noses with her. Eskimo kiss. Then plants his lips on hers. Wipes his mouth.

"You don't need the lipstick you know." Your lips are already beautiful. "And the people around here are traditional, they associate obvious make up with…"

"Whores?"

"A certain kind of woman. I know that's not you, but they don't."

"But what if I am Max?," she says, her hands on his wrists. "What if I have the spirit of a whore? What if I like the idea of being a courtesan, with men in her thrall? What if it sounds like freedom?"

He laughs, in his speaking voice. Not his real laugh.

"Oh you're sweet," he says. "But I know you Lili. You dress trendy, you talk tough, but you're full of nothing but love. Your heart is so big and you've been searching. You've always been so alone, and looking for someone to love and now you have me."

"I wasn't always alone."

"You were. Your soul was alone. Spiritually alone – until I found you. And so was I. When my wife died I thought I would never find love again. I was lost. Empty. But you saved me Lili. We saved each other."

She looks over her shoulder, and I think, for a moment, that she sees me. I look into her eyes, so blue they're almost navy. She is beautiful. A little younger than me. Not by much.

"What is it?"

"Nothing, nothing, just the wind."

They slip back into French, or Franglais. I only catch every other word. Then he pushes her back on the bed. Her hands slip around his waist, up to his shoulders, she lifts him off her to unbutton his shirt. No Lili, no, he likes to do that himself. Or to leave it on. You can't know that yet. He moves her hands away and kisses her, pushes her back down. I watch them make love in the room that used to be mine. I have been erased. A straight line of history now, an emptiness of Max from the death of his wife in the England he couldn't bear, to Lili here today. I was never here.

Unless I am the wife. We never married, but maybe I am the dead wife in this story. Maybe he wasn't married to the wife in the story he told me either. Maybe there was no wife. Maybe there were many wives. When I fell what happened? When my body hit the ground outside. What then? I came to sit by the window with my hiccups, but what was happening outside this room? Did I go to hospital? Did I die on the cobblestones? Am I even dead? Am I still sleeping, anonymous in some Italian hospital, named or unnamed. Does Max visit me? Did anyone know I was here with him? Am I buried? Did I burn? Was there a funeral? Was it written up in the newspaper as a terrible accident? A mysterious disappearance? Am I in some unmarked grave beyond the city? Am I under water? In a forest? Was I ever here? Or did I pass through, unnoticed, a stranger, light as ash?

When they finish he gets up immediately. She gathers the sheets around her. He buttons his trousers and smooths his hair. He looks at the clock. He leaves the room then comes back with a drink. Two glasses with sparkling liquid, on clear one cloudy – brandy and lemonade. This, at least is the same. He puts the cloudy glass down beside her, strokes her cheek with the back of his knuckle. His hands are rough as a cat's tongue, although the rest of him is smooth. He sits back and watches her as he sips on his clear liquid. She drinks, she starts to talk to him in French again. He answers in monosyllables. He is scrolling through his phone. He stands up, he gives her a kiss, and he leaves the room. She sits up, the duvet gathered at her chest covering her breasts even though she doesn't know anyone can see her. She drains the last of the drink.

She hiccups.

Her flesh is creamy pale. In Italy at this time of year, she ought to be browned or burned. Her skin speaks of the inside of rooms and closed top cars, of recycled air, of sitting still and waiting. Waiting like Penelope waited for Odysseus, dutifully weaving and unweaving the same threads.

She reaches through me. Her arm passes right through. I don't feel a thing. She unhooks the shutters and lets them swing open, crashing against the walls. She gets up and attaches them to the hooks on the walls either side. I did this too. A drunk or suicidal woman does not hook the shutters onto the walls. She sits back on the bed and closes her eyes, lets the breeze I can't feel come into the room, cut through the sticky post-sex sweat. Then she stands up and walks to the window, looks out at the street. I look with her. It's a long time since I saw the street. Or any street.

Peach and peppermint coloured buildings, with bubbles of peeling paint. Twisted iron rails on balconies. Silk knickers fluttering on lines. A policeman on a moped, winding his way around parked cars. A group of young men, brown arms in short sleeved white shirts, arguing or just chatting. Two laughing women with ice-creams and backpacks. A skinny cat curls around a doorway then disappears. One of the men looks up, sees her: bare shouldered and smudge-lipped standing in the open window.

"Ciao Bella!" he shouts

She shrugs a shoulder, blows a kiss

"Ciao!"

Then she withdraws back into the room. Shuts the shutters again. She hiccups again. And swears. And holds her breath. Trying to get rid of them that way, I suppose. I see her future laid out before me. I don't know if she still imagines she will see Guadaloupe, or France, or England, or anywhere else. I don't know if she thinks she will see any more of Italy again other than what lies just outside this window, where she is framed like a painting. I don't know if she'll fall. Or if she'll jump. Or if he'll push her. If the drinks don't do the trick he'll have to push. Maybe he intends to keep her, for her beautiful shoulders, or her father's money, or maybe his plan is always to kill us. But she could still escape. She's still alive. She can still throw the shutters open and feel the breeze and flirt with boys.

If I'd done that. If I'd been braver. If I hadn't drunk so much. If I'd walked away. If I'd been less in love. Less naïve. If I'd had less faith that things would get better. If his hair was less silky. I could leave this room. I could travel for real. I could be free to go anywhere. Like she is.

I wonder if. I wonder if I still could? Can myself slip inside her? Can I walk away? Could I live in this body, now mine is lost somewhere? This slim waist, this soft skin? Could I slip it on like a blue silk blouse and with a new beauty, a new daring, walk away?

I kneel in front of her. I focus on her eyes, her lips. I am light, but there is a force within me. A determination. If you can dream it you can be it. Don't dream it, be it. Was that from a film? Or just some cheesy fridge magnet. I push my lightness into the space she occupies. I feel myself filling her out.

I think of yoga classes again. Meditations. The teacher saying "Imagine a light entering your body and spreading out down every limb, every nerve, every blood vessel."

I am the light. I spread out around her neck over the top of her head around her eyes, down each arm into the tip of each finger. She breathes me in and I fill up her belly, her diaphragm.

No more hiccups. I am the light and I'm here to calm you.

In my own time I flicker my eyes open, reborn. It's no different looking through blue eyes than it is through brown ones. I look around at the room, from inside my new body. I raise a hand up through the air. The air has weight. It's sticky and slow. The breeze is pointed and fresh as lemon zest. I run a hand over my new right thigh. It's slightly stubbled with spikes of dark hair. The blonde isn't natural then.

There is not much time. I open drawers and throw on clothes. Shorts, a long-sleeved kaftan, a baseball cap, sunglasses. I look around for a handbag. I find only a tiny clutch on the dresser, with a lipstick and some tampons, and an empty folded tote from some museum. I go to Max's side of the bed with the little chest of drawers. I tip it forward. The front of the draws is thick and I don't know how to pick a lock, but the back of the cabinet is shoddy MDF. He wouldn't expect so much violence from either of us, but dead women know what it takes. We don't hang about. With a pair of nail scissors I stab at the flimsy wood until a hole forms, and then I tear strips off until I'm inside. There's cash in envelopes. Different currencies. I stuff it all into the museum tote. A blue cardboard folder – passports – my own, faded with a picture of my face six years ago, young and blank as a ghost. Useless now, but I take it anyway. Then hers – it turns out she's Swiss, which surprises me. I wonder if I can speak French now. Does language sit in the body? Do I have any others?

I take her passport. It's a shame Max's isn't here or I would take that too. I do find an assortment of other passports, mostly for women, but a few for men – the male ones have pictures of Max at different ages, with different names. I take those. I also take the credit cards I find. I might not be able to use them, but why make it easy for him to come after us?

We leave the room. I run her down the stairs. It feels like driving a car, although it's a long time since I did that, I'm in control but the parameters of what I'm controlling aren't quite part of me. I feel the slap of her sandals on each step as a distant sensation. It's like virtual reality. I hear our breathing quick and sharp, the flutter of a foreign heart in my chest, praying Max will not be coming the other way, thinking of an excuse, a run to the shop, something dropped from the window? When my voice comes out who will he hear? Me or her?

We make it down the empty stairwell, I throw open the door, and the world hits me in the face like a steam oven. It's still afternoon and the sun is bright through my sunglasses. It's a world I haven't seen for a long time. A country I never got to see properly, but I must resist the urge to delay. I can always come back one day. If I can just escape now, I can go wherever I like, forever. When this body dies, I can jump to a new one, a new one after that, keep going, keep living, forever.

Just run. Don't look too suspicious. Slow down. Don't look anxious. Don't draw attention. Don't look around too much but stay aware. Cross the road to avoid that group of men. Hunch. Don't look beautiful. But don't look vulnerable either. Look like you know where you're headed. Walk like you own the street.

"Ciao Bella!"

Not that much.

I turn corners, and corners and corners. I don't know where I'm going yet. I just need to get far away from where Max thinks I am. Buy some time. I find a crowd. Tourists. A cacophony of languages. Smells of panini, gelato, sunscreen and sweat. I spot a paper map, dropped on the ground, pick it up and examine it. I stand next to four chattering women around my age, trying to look like part of their group, as I try and remember the shape of the streets I've run along to get here, get a sense of my location, somewhere I might find an airport bus or a train station.

"Hiccup"

Something inside me. My diaphragm moves.

"Look up."

I don't want to look up. My face might be seen. But the command comes from inside.

"Lookup"

She's still here. I've pushed her back, but she's still there in the pit of my stomach. We're in this body together, and I'm not sure I'm welcome but maybe she wants to get away as much as I do. We can fight for control later.

I look up. And there's what I wanted, from Rome.

Towering above me, all the Gods with their beautiful curled beards. The muscled thighs and chests. The water running over beautiful waving hair, over muscles that seemed to flex in the light. They say the devil is a handsome man, but the Gods aren't half bad either. Our stomach somersaults. I feel the familiar flush of hormones, warming through all my limbs, tickling at the underside of my skin. I feel like a teenager again, watching a boyband, shirts ripped off, strategically hosed down for the video. Oh, Max is this why you didn't want me here? You aren't the only man with beautiful hair!

I came here to Italy and then never saw the Trevi Fountain until now. None of those bucket list things I was seeking. I was here months and Max always said he would bring me here one day. When the weather was good. When it wasn't tourist season. When he wasn't busy. No it wasn't safe to go alone. Italian men are predators. Especially on naïve young British girls.

"I'm not naïve," I said

I was. I didn't want to be. And I thought coming to Italy would make me less so. Eventually it worked. I tear my gaze from the chiselled abs. No time for men. No time for sex. No time for sightseeing of any kind not now, not yet. One day soon. A train seems sensible. It will be harder to escape, if he does happen to catch me. But there are more places to hide. I trace the streets to the nearest metro station. The map tells me a train to the airport. I set off, it's just a five minute walk, then I can duck underground. Weave through the crowds. Then run up against the turnstiles. I don't know how to buy a ticket. I don't know which ticket I need. Or how to use it. I should have bought a guide book somewhere. An Idiot's Guide to Italy or something. Slipped into a tourist shop. There are instructions in English on the machine but I can't make sense of them. The only train tickets I ever bought were in England, where I walked up to a desk in a town centre station and told them where I wanted to be. But this is Europe, right? The transport system crosses borders, it must be similar country to country. And easier, if you speak some of the language. Swiss people are renowned for being good linguists right? She spoke French, but maybe she speaks Italian too?

I bend over in the corner so my head is down, I pretend to fiddle with my bag. I close my eyes. I turn myself inwards.

"Lili?" I try and say it down into my diaphragm. For some reason that's where I feel she is. A trapped breath. "Lilli. Are you still here?"

I wait. I try to quiet my mind like in the meditation sessions I went to long ago searching for inner peace. Let your mind be like a still pool into which the universe can drop stones of wisdom. Lili drop a pebble. The water ripples. It hisses like the wind.

"Get the hell out of my body bitch."

"No, shhsh, Lili, I'm sorry…"

"Get out. I don't know who you are buit…"

"Lili, I'm sorry. I should have asked permission. I didn't know how."

"This body is mine. You can't have it."

"But Max can?"

"What?"

"Max. He tries to tell you what to do. He tries to keep you in that hotel room. He tries to tell you what to wear."

"I do whatever I like. I travel with him. He's not my keeper."

"Is that true? Were you going to ask your father for money like he asked?"

"For us. For our future. My Dad has plenty of money."

"Is it your future though? Or is just his? That business venture – do you even know what it is? Do you even know what he does?"

"I don't need to know…" she sounds less certain.

"He had your passport and credit cards locked up in a safe. Did you have the key?"

I feel her flip over in my belly

"You were there. You saw all of those passports. You saw mine. See?" I get my passport out of the bag, hold my picture, my name up to our eyes. "That's me. He took my passport. He took my money. He persuaded me it wasn't safe to go out. He stopped me learning Italian. He promised to show me the world and I spent months trapped in a tiny apartment. He gave me a drink that made me sleepy and lethargic, then one day I fell out of the window. Maybe he even pushed me. And what do you think happened to those other women in those other passport pictures? Did he tell you about his dead wife? How many dead wives do you think there are?"

"The drinks?"

"Yes. That's what made you hiccup. Made your brain foggy. Tell me you didn't used to feel more alive before you came here?"

"You can't have my body. This is mine. I'm sorry for what happened, but this is mine."

"I need you Lili. We need to work together. I've got you out of the apartment before it was too late. By the time you realised yourself you would have been too far gone. But now I need your help. I don't know how to buy a train ticket. I don't speak Italian. Can you help? Get us to the airport. We'll fly to England together, get beyond his reach – then I'll find a way out of this I promise. We just need to ride together a while, and we need to do it fast. He might already realise we're gone."

"OK. OK. Be quiet then. Give me my brain back."

I don't know quite what to do, but I try to curl up into a ball of what's left of me. I settle into the back of her brain, with just one soul-eye poking out watching what she's doing through a tiny hole, a periscope. It's like watching a film, in a foreign language, on a shitty TV, with a terrible signal. And my hands tied behind my back. At least I know what's happening. At least I consented to it.

"Sorry I didn't warn you before I took over." I whispered to her.

"Shush."

Her fingers skim over the various buttons of the ticket machine. I notice she uses the French language setting, so that must be her mother tongue. I'm glad it's not English – if we're both going to be living here then there's no point us having the same default language. She smoothly walks through the turnstiles, apologises in Italian to someone she brushes a little too close to. She boards the train, stays standing even though there are seats available. That's good, she knows she needs to be able to see up and down the carriage, to be able to move quickly. She swings off the train when it reaches the airport, heads to the departures board to look for flights leaving in a few hours. Something with time still to buy tickets but that won't leave us hanging around. If I stay still, if I try and calm my mind and get receptive, I can hear her thoughts. I can feel they're in French, but because I'm inside I can recognise the gist of them, watch them, more like pictures or sensations. There are a lot of possible destinations.

"It needs to be Europe. Somewhere where I won't need a visa, where I can just enter. France."

"No. He knows you'll be comfortable there. Nowhere French speaking. Not for now. And not Switzerland either."

"Ha. Over my dead body. Erm – sorry. Where then?"

"England."

"Really?" I feel her wrinkle our nose.

I hate England as much as anyone but her disgust offends me.

"I have a flat there. Max persuaded me to rent it out so we could travel on the income. With any luck it's still in my name. The rent went to our joint bank account but it was in my name. And we never married so it won't have been easy for him to take ownership. We can sell it. Then we can run wherever we like with that money."

"We? You think you're staying in my body?"

"You want to go back to your Daddy for money?"

"I'll get a job."

I uncurl, I grow myself big, stretch out so I fill her up completely. Then I walk over to the vending machine, buy a can of cola, shake it up, open it and let the liquid fizz all over that nice blue shirt and jeans. Then I shrink back down, just a little.

"You bitch!"

A few people turn around to look.

"Stop drawing attention to us."

"You can talk."

"Look. I'm on your side. I wanted to rescue you. I didn't want to see another woman fall out of that window. I don't want Max to keep doing this. But I don't want to stay dead either. He's not going to do that to

me any more than he's going to do it to you. So we're going to have to come to some arrangement. Alternate days, whatever. I don't care, but I'm here now and I'm not going to leave you alone."

She's on her phone, buying a ticket to Heathrow. She almost buys two.

"I can't deal with you being in my body with me."

"I can stay quiet. On your days I'll just curl up. Leave you in peace."

"I'll know you're there. When I'm peeing."

"That's what you're worried about?"

"Not exclusively no. I get it. You don't want to die. I can sympathise. But this body is occupied. In use. We need to get you a new one."

"A new one? How…"

"Would you object to being a man?"

I've thought about it often. The freedom to walk down streets at night, to sit with my legs apart on buses, to drink alone in bars, to not bleed every month for half my life. I wouldn't mind giving it a try.

"Go on?"

"How about we head back to the city? How about we send Max out of that window. How about at the crucial moment you enter his body? And you get to do whatever you like with it?"

I imagine it. Having that soft skin, and silky hair, all for myself, all for my own.

"Deal."

Holly Barratt is a writer living in Wales who primarily writes short stories in the science fiction, horror and magic realism genres. We first published her in our Call of the Wyld anthology (available now from bookshops, from Amazon or our website www.wyldblood.com). She is currently working on a novel.

The Gun that Killed Certainty James (and Other Collectible Oddities)

D.K. Latta

When I was fourteen, my best friend was a kid named Larry Banncle.

My family had moved to a town about 100 kilometres North-East of Toronto. It was the middle of the school semester; I was the new kid in town and Larry was on the watch for a pal -- like a hawk looking for a rustle in the grass. He was a bit of an odd one, Larry was: awkward, poorly dressed. He tended to smell a little. I think it was Groucho Marx who said: "I don't want to belong to any club that would have me as a member." But when you're the new kid in town you accept what you can get. Even when you know the kid who's the first to befriend you is only doing so because no one who already knows him will have anything to do with him.

We didn't really have the same tastes in TV shows, teachers, girls.

What Larry did have was the most amazing collection I had ever seen. Rather,

his dad did. The Banncle house was crammed with stuff. That's the best way I can describe it: "stuff." It wasn't like Mr. Banncle was into stamps, or rare tools, or even porcelain dolls. No, he collected anything. The house was what I imagined the back rooms of P.T. Barnum's museum would've looked like in the 19th Century -- the areas roped off from the public, awaiting cataloguing.

There wasn't a Mrs. Banncle. Larry didn't say what happened to her and I never asked. That's not what boys do.

So I'd come back to Larry's house in that interregnum between the end of the school day and the beginning of dinner -- too much time to sit idle, not enough to do anything worth doing. This being the days before video games and Xboxes, when "Gilligan's Island" reruns and game shows overwhelmed the television. We'd wander through the house, daylight through the curtains glancing off dust motes in the air, Larry showing off this artefact or that.

He hoisted a pistol one day. I shifted nervously, equal parts boyish fascination with anything weapon related, and sober realization that, NRA slogans aside, guns really do kill people. Particularly when wielded nonchalantly by a fourteen year old.

"This," Larry explained, "is the gun that killed Certainty James." The late afternoon sunlight raced along the barrel like mercury as Larry tilted it one way and then the other.

"Neat," I said, hypnotized. The gun gleamed like it had just come from the factory. It seemed an odd design; weird engravings along one side and a little knob where the hammer should be. But, then, all I knew about guns was from "Gunsmoke" reruns. "That must've cost a fortune."

Larry shrugged, as though such thoughts were trifling. He straightened his skinny arm, as though taking aim. The gun bobbed like a cork in water and he relented and crooked his elbow a bit, to better take the weight. Then he dropped it to his side and said, "Wanna hold it?" as though playing with a gun was beneath him.

I hesitated, knowing the talking I'd receive if my parents were to hear about it. Then I said, equally indifferent, "Sure, why not?" It was heavy, not like the guns I used to make out of Lego. "Who was Certainty James?"

"Oh, um, he was an old outlaw or somethin'," he mumbled, leafing through other items on one of the shelves, as though disinterested in the conversation. I suppressed a grin, realizing Larry had no idea. Presumably his father had once told him the gun had killed Certainty James and, primping like a peacock, Larry was proud to demonstrate knowledge he didn't possess. A couple of years earlier boasting our dads knew something we didn't would have been enough. But now we were fourteen and our dads were something we merely tolerated.

Still, I was maturing enough that I let him have his face saving moment. I simply nodded and carefully laid the gun back on the table. Larry was already holding up a jewelled egg that he claimed was by Fabergé – but I figured had to be a replica.

Still at least that was someone I had actually heard of.

That gun kind of piqued my curiosity. Oh, I didn't doubt I could ask my mother who was Certainty James and she'd tell me, maybe even name some old bio pic starring Tyrone Power. But in those halcyon pre-internet years I wanted to find out on my own.

The school library's file cards turned up nothing, however. So I leafed through books about outlaws of the American west -- the name having a kind of cowboy ring to it. But to no avail. Then I tried books about gangsters of the 1920s and '30s. I next took my research to the public library, expanding my scope to include notorious Canadians from the Black Donnelly's to "Red" Ryan, and to British highwaymen and Australian outlaws. Yet nowhere did the name Certainty James appear.

So the next time I was at Larry's house I went with an agenda.

As we wandered through the motley collection of knickknacks, oddities, and genuine antiquities, Larry equal parts tour guide and fellow explorer, I made sure to direct us toward the table with the gun. As Larry was leafing through a mint copy of *Dime Comics* #1 -- making snarky comments about the story and art as fourteen year olds do -- I looked for any manufacturer's mark, or at least to imprint its unusual design in my brain to compare to pictures in a gun book I had checked out of the library. I figured if I could identify the gun with an era or country, I might place Certainty James. As I reached to pick it up a voice snapped:

"Don't touch that!"

We both jumped, Larry dropping his comic, clearly half afraid that was the forbidden object. Mr. Banncle stood in a doorway. The room behind him was dark, which was why we assumed he wasn't home.

"S-sorry," we stammered together.

Mr. Banncle wasn't an intimidating man. His hair was thinning, his features regular, his eyes always seeming a bit tired. He perpetually wore suits, though I wasn't sure what he did for a living. It wasn't until that moment that it occurred to me how little he looked like Larry.

No, he wasn't intimidating, but nonetheless he had an air of authority about him, particularly when you're caught going through his things in his house. His eyes stayed focused on me. "You're...Perry? Is that right?"

I nodded.

"Well, guns aren't toys -- you're old enough to know that."

I could feel Larry relax as he realized it was I, not he, who had transgressed.

"Sorry," I said, a little hoarsely. Then, hoping to salvage some respectability from this, said, "Larry said it was the gun that killed Certainty James and I'd been doing a bit of research on-" I started to say "he," then "she," then settled for "-on Certainty James. I thought it'd make a good school project." I hadn't really intended anything of the sort, but as I said it, I realized it might be a good idea. Teachers were always throwing assignments at us and it wouldn't hurt to have something researched and prepped, waiting in the wings.

"How do you know about Certainty James?" asked Mr. Banncle sharply, suspiciously.

"I, uh, didn't know anything...until Larry showed me the gun."

He stared at me for a moment, then stepped into the room. He had been so still that I actually jumped a little, almost as though I'd forgotten that he could move. He picked up the gun, looked at it for a moment -- then slipped it into his pocket. "I think there are better topics a bright kid like you could study." He started from the room, then stopped in the doorway. "Ask your friend if he's staying for dinner, Larry." Then he vanished back into the darkness.

Needless to say, I told Larry I had to get home.

When you're young you tend to romanticize everything. So you can imagine what theories and narratives wove themselves through my brain about the gun that Mr. Banncle didn't want me touching. What if Certainty James wasn't some ancient outlaw, but a 1960s radical or something (they probably had nicknames like Certainty, too, I surmised)? Maybe that's why the history books didn't mention him (or her) -- I was looking too far back. Maybe Mr. Banncle had that gun because *he* had killed Certainty James, and had fled up to Canada with those draft dodgers a few years before, changed his name, and tried to hide the gun in plain sight among his collection. He just hadn't counted on his son befriending Encyclopedia Brown -- namely, me. It almost made sense. Well, at least to a fourteen year old with an active imagination.

It would certainly explain the car watching their house.

The Banncle house was on the outskirts of town, sitting back from one of those roads whose name becomes a number as it leaves the municipal limits. Across the road from the houses was a fallow field of tall grass -- in all the time I lived there, I never saw any farmer ploughing it.

I can't say when the black sedan first appeared, parked beside the road a few lots down from the Banncle place. Perhaps I rode my bike past it a few times without giving it much thought. But when it did catch my attention, it stayed. It looked too clean, like something someone had just driven off a rental lot. And it had tinted windows so you couldn't see inside.

Given my suspicions about Mr. Banncle -- which even I knew was more fancy than genuine conviction -- seeing a mysterious black car in the area was oil to my imaginative fire.

I was wandering through one of the rooms of the Banncle house, my hands kept determinedly in my pockets ever since Mr. Banncle's admonishment. Larry had gone for a drink or something -- I can't remember now. But I was alone. And then I wasn't as Mr. Banncle stood in the doorway.

"Perry, right?" he asked.

I nodded, though I doubted Larry brought enough kids around that it should be hard to remember my name. Mr. Banncle's uncertainty about my identity might have indicated how little he cared about who his son hung out with, but I thought it was more an indication of how he seemed perpetually preoccupied.

"You like my collection?"

I nodded, then shrugged -- in my 14-year-old-way not wanting to seem egregiously enthusiastic. "I collect comic books," I said. "I keep the important ones bagged," I told him hastily, just so he wouldn't think I was a nerd.

He nodded, only half listening. "I used to collect a lot of things."

I thought that was odd to say given we were in a house so full of junk it probably violated fire codes. Then I realized I hadn't seen anything that struck me as a new addition to the collection in all the weeks I had known Larry. Was this a museum to a dead hobby? "You don't collect anymore?"

He picked up a little cameo that had a picture of a woman I thought might have been Queen Victoria. A slight smile quirked his lips, as though reminiscing, and I suddenly realized I had never seen him smile before. Even now, it was brief -- a remnant, like the items in the house. "I used to collect keepsakes. It was about all I was allowed in my job. I wasn't supposed to do anything else. Technically, even pocketing the occasional memento is forbidden, but it's a minor infraction...compared to other things."

"What...do you do? Larry's never said."

"I was a researcher. I studied places, people...times."

"You're a historian?" I said, suddenly putting this eccentric collection in a context.

He smiled again, that brief, sad little smile. "Something like that."

I knew he was being deliberately coy, but wasn't sure why or in what way.

"But what's the point of researching, if you never let it impact on you? Surely study is supposed to alter the studier? Otherwise, you're not even human, are you?"

I stared blankly, having no idea what he was talking about, or what I should say, but aware that he clearly wanted to talk to someone. Otherwise, why would he be talking to a fourteen year old whose name he had to struggle to remember? And then something else occurred to me. Whatever he wanted to talk about, he clearly couldn't talk about it with Larry.

"There was one...subject I was researching," he said quietly, idly sorting through objects on a table. "A minor footnote in history. A loathsome little man, a killer and thief and coward. I was to make a few entries on him -- the weather on the morning he was gunned down, that sort of stuff. But then I decided to go back further. After all, history isn't just about what, but why. Why did he kill the bank clerk, but not the security guard? Little things like that that you couldn't understand simply from studying the day he died."

I cocked my head. "Are we talking about Certainty James?"

He looked at me sharply. "Where did you hear that name?"

"Larry showed me the gun -- remember?"

He stared at me blankly for a moment, then nodded, as if finally placing my face. "Right. That was you. I'm sorry. I've seen too many faces, it's hard to keep them straight."

Just then Larry returned, hovering at the threshold, unsure if he was interrupting something. If he was, Mr. Banncle didn't show it. Instead, he reached out, tousled his son's hair with an affection I had rarely seen from him and excused himself. But as he started to leave, he stopped and turned back. "We should talk some more...Perry." And then he was gone.

As I rode my bike back home, I noticed the black car again.

A few days after that oblique conversation I rode out to Larry's place once again. I remember it was a windy day, making it hard to stay on my bike. The sky was a watery grey, but with a rampart of blackness on the horizon that meant a storm. At least, that's how I remember it.

As I approached the black car, parked in what had almost become its accustomed place, I was startled when the passenger door creaked open and a man stepped out onto the road. He wore a bright yellow overcoat, cinched so tight at the waist that it exaggerated his shoulders, almost like a zoot suit out of a Spy vs. Spy cartoon. He was bald, and his eyes were hidden by wraparound sunglasses blacker than any sunglasses I'd ever seen. He held up a hand and grinned. "Oh, boy," he said. "Boy -- may I speak with you a moment?"

I skidded my bike to a halt before him, frowning.

"I would like to ask you a question or two. Is that okay with you?" his words had an accent I couldn't place. And though his lips continued to smile, I had the feeling the smile didn't continue up into those hidden eyes.

"I'm not supposed to talk with strangers." Normally I was happy to present myself as older and mature. But for some reason I was grateful to play the minor card.

"Yes, yes," he said, as if agreeing and not really listening all at the same time. He pulled his wallet from his pocket and flipped it open. It was a badge. At least, that's what I perceived it as being. Yet I couldn't really tell you what it said, or what it looked like. For some reason my eyes ached, and I felt a headache start to rise at the back of my neck. I looked away and he quickly closed his wallet and dropped it back into his pocket. I swayed there a moment, dizzy. The rear door of the car was open, but I couldn't recall seeing him reach for it. And suddenly I was sitting in the back seat, but with no memory of getting in, or even having dismounted from my bike. It was almost as though time was kind of folding around me. Instead of experiencing continuous events, I was just getting the creases. I felt nauseous. The bald man was in the front seat, twisted around to look at me. The driver never turned around.

"Yes, now, we have quick talk, then you be on your way." With that badge I thought maybe he might be a government agent. I told myself the accent was Québécois -- but I knew it wasn't. "We are interested in finding a man. You visiting this neighbourhood a lot, so perhaps you can help. We are looking for man named Banncle. You have seen this man?"

I blinked at him, my tongue feeling dry in my mouth.

"Do you know of this Banncle?"

Disoriented, nonetheless I knew what to say. "No."

His smile dropped from his lips. Not so much like he was angry, just unsure. He glanced at his companion, then back at me. "You visit house down the road."

"Larry's house," I said, realizing it was best to stick to the truth. "My friend Larry."

"There is boy in house?" This time he leaned over to his friend and whispered something. I couldn't understand the words, but I knew it wasn't French. Then he turned back to me. "And what is Larry's last name?"

"Larry," I said. "Just...Larry."

He started to ask me something more, but I said, "I'm feeling really sick -- I think I'm going to puke." And I wasn't lying. The bald man looked at his companion, then back at me. And suddenly once again there was that disorienting shift, that sense of folding. There was light and the door was open, as though I'd blinked and missed it swinging wide.

Then I was on my bike. Then I was alone on the road, watching dust kicked up by the black car as it drove away. I teetered for a moment, grateful for the buffeting wind and the way it cleared my head, pushing down the nausea in my stomach. But the whole experience had left me unnerved, even as it was rapidly seeming almost like just a dream.

I decided not to visit Larry that day and turned my bike around.

On the way home, the dark clouds caught up with me, and I was drenched by a massive downpour before I rode up my driveway. In the night I started vomiting and by morning I had a fever. The reasonable explanation was that I had caught the flu in the rain. The unreasonable explanation was that my encounter with the men, and that weird disorientation, hadn't sat well with my system. Whatever the cause, I was home from school for two days.

On the third day my mother packed me a lunch and waved me off to school.

I didn't go.

Instead, I biked to the Banncle place. There was no black car along the road as I approached, but I didn't really believe my prevarication had sent them on their way. I braked in the middle of the road and stood up on the pedals, hovering for a moment as I looked over the fallow field. I half expected to see a bald head and wrap around dark glasses poke up from the stalks of tall grass. The bike lost its balance and I put out a foot to steady myself. After another moment, hearing only the breeze and the distant caw of crows, I pedalled on to the Banncle house.

Dropping my bike on the lawn I mounted the creaking wood steps. I knocked, but there was no answer. I wandered around to the back of the house. Mr. Banncle was seated on the back porch, a cup of coffee at his side. In his lap he had what looked like a small open briefcase -- except he was typing in it as though it were a typewriter. Remembering back now, it could almost have been a laptop.

But we didn't have those then. He heard me before he saw me, and quickly closed it. "Can I help you?"

For the first time I noticed a slight lilt to his words, as though Mr. Banncle also had an accent, though not as noticeable as the man in the car. Then he squinted at me. "You're Larry's friend? Larry isn't here. I guess he'll be home any minute," he said. And I realized that seeing me, he must have assumed school was over for the day. It reminded me of how distracted Mr. Banncle always seemed, that he wouldn't realize what time it was.

"Yeah, I know he's not here. But you said we should talk some more."

He frowned, having forgotten our conversation, and his momentary vulnerability. "Did I?"

"Yeah, about...about Certainty James."

He stiffened, like a cat when it hears a noise and instantly becomes alert. Then he breathed out, like a cat relaxing, as it identified the phantom sound as non-threatening. "That's right."

"You said that studying history isn't any good if you remain, I dunno, untouched by it."

Slowly, he nodded. "You stop being human."

I sat down on a chair opposite him. I had made the decision not to leave until I understood what was going on. Why Mr. Banncle seemed so troubled. Why he had a house full of junk. Why men seemed to be looking for him. So I just waited, letting him understand I wasn't going anywhere until someone said something.

"Certainty James was an inconsequential figure," he began, at last. "Even by outlaw standards he was a third stringer. But sometimes those make the best studies, as they haven't been strip mined by other academics -- so to speak. But the more I studied him, the more I went back into his past to make sense of the choices that led him to that wasted, psychotic life and that fateful showdown outside Tal Gruberman's General

Store -- the more I saw the choices weren't always his. Once upon a time he was a boy like any -- like you. With as much potential for good as for bad. And maybe if his mother hadn't died, and his father hadn't beat him, and those other kids hadn't..." His voice trailed off. "I'd spent all my professional life studying history, documenting it, filing abstract dissertations. But Certainty James was abused, and abused others, and died a pointless inconsequential death. And I was just going to write about it. And I thought: didn't that make me as bad as those who abused him? As bad as he was when he gunned down people in cold blood? Maybe instead of just studying history, I was obligated to see if it could be made better. Maybe that was the true way to learn about causality, about consequences.

"A man once wrote, or will write -- I'm not sure anymore -- he wrote that those who forget history will repeat it. But I began to think that those who studied history and accepted it as inevitable were guilty of something far worse: complicity. But that violated every rule of my profession. And I understand the danger of the domino effect, that if you interfere on too great a scale, the repercussions could be -- well, who knows? But Certainty James was such a minor, irrelevant figure." His voice faded for a moment. Then he nodded curtly, as though to himself. "I knew if I were to pursue this new course I would, in effect, become an outlaw on a scale greater that Certainty James ever was. I could never stop running. Literally...*never*." He sighed after that and stared unseeing at his back yard. Then he said, "Larry is not my biological son -- you understand that, right?"

I hadn't. I hadn't understood any of what he was telling me -- or not telling me. But then, as he said that, it was a little like the sun peaking from behind a storm front that you thought was never going to end. I could picture Larry as a troubled kid, rescued from a violent dad and abusive playmates by a

stranger, a historian -- but not a historian as we understood the term. Slowly, I nodded.

He muttered something that I had to strain to hear: "It will be for later academics to assess the consequences of what I've done, to judge. I'm now a part of events, and can no longer put them in perspective."

I sat quietly for a moment, staring at my frayed sneakers. I wasn't really sure if I understood everything, the concepts knocking at the door of my thoughts. I wasn't sure if I opened that door whether it would let in wonder and understanding, or whether it would drive me insane. So I simply said, "There's a car that's been hanging around. They were asking about you."

Mr. Banncle sat up rigid. "What?"

"I told them I hadn't heard of you," I said, afraid he was going to accuse me. But he was barely aware I was there. He looked around a bit wildly.

"Where's Larry? Why isn't he home yet?"

"It's still early," I said. "I skipped school to come see you."

This seemed to reassure him, at least a little. He nodded, then stood. "You'd better go now -- I have things to do." Without even looking at me, he went into the house and closed the door.

I didn't go to school that day. I didn't want to have to explain why I was late. Because I had already been sick, no one at the school thought to call my parents about my absenteeism.

The next day I did go to school, determined to talk to Larry, to see if Mr. Banncle -- the man who wasn't really his father -- had said anything to him about my visit. But Larry wasn't at school that day.

Thinking about Mr. Banncle's panic on hearing about the black car, and wondering about Larry's absence, I could barely keep my mind on my work. I didn't volunteer to answer any questions and those I was called upon for I got wrong. Eventually the end of day bell rang and I was on my bike racing out to the Banncle place. As I pumped my legs faster than I ever had before, I tried to make sense of what I had been told and seen and experienced. Men with strange accents. Academics who researched history. And one who could no longer just be objective. Mr. Banncle said Certainty James had been irrelevant, but he had also talked of dominoes. Of unforeseen repercussions. I thought of a gun that resembled no gun that had ever been made. A history that no longer was.

I skidded up the gravel driveway and sent my bike clattering onto its side as I bounded up the wood steps. I pounded on the door, panic welling up inside me, though I couldn't be sure why. When the door opened, I felt a momentary relief.

But only a momentary one.

The dark haired woman in the doorway I had never seen before. She looked at me with a mixture of politeness and suspicion. "Yes?" she asked.

For a moment I couldn't speak, then I said, "Uh, is Larry around?"

"I'm afraid there's no one here by that name."

"Are you...Mrs. Banncle?"

She smiled indulgently and shook her head. "You must have the wrong address."

Over her shoulder I could see a perfectly ordinary living room. The museum of uncatalogued junk was nowhere to be seen. I looked frantically around at the lawn, but saw no "For Sale" sign. "Did...did they move?"

"We've been here three months -- I'm not sure of the name of the people who were here before. I really think someone must have given you the wrong address." Her smile was more brittle now, as though wondering if I was playing a prank. "You'll have to excuse me now." Politely, but firmly, she closed the door.

I stood there for a moment, sweat trickling down my ribs that had little to do with the exertion of riding my bike. I had been here just yesterday, yet this woman was claiming she had been here months. I stumbled down the steps. In my mind I was thinking about the black car, about the sense of time folding around me. I wondered if it was possible to fold events around, to erase certain things, to rearrange events. To make it so someone never lived in a house that you knew they had lived in.

As I picked up my bike in fingers that felt tingly and thick, I was distracted by the cough of an engine. I looked around and saw the rear lights of what looked to be a black car disappearing in a swirl of road dust.

Strangely seeing that, I almost felt relieved. I couldn't be sure it was the same car. But if it was, then maybe that meant that Mr. Banncle and Larry had got away, had gone somewhere else. The men in the black car were still looking for them.

The next day in school I didn't bother asking anyone about Larry -- I was pretty sure I'd be met with blank stares. When attendance was called, the teacher went from Bailey to Bryers without missing a beat.

No one I've ever met in all the years since has ever heard of Certainty James. I never saw Larry Banncle again.

D.K. Latta has been writing fiction, mostly of the speculative fiction variety, off and on for over two decades, as well as occasional non-fiction reviews and essays about movies, graphic novels, and pop culture. He lives in Canada.

The Ping
David Matthews

My lawyer says I should keep this short and sweet. Full of words like 'amicable', 'moving on', 'resilience'. The kind of words we use to show we're nice stable adults, the kind of people who can be hurt, but not too much.

By the time you read this, a computer will already have sentiment mined my text and spat out a judgement for you to rubber stamp, she says. Best keep it full of positivity and contrition, so the system gives me a good score. You're probably about to go on lunch. You just want to read a couple of paragraphs and click on "confirm recommendation" or whatever and eat a chicken sandwich and some crisps and scroll through your phone.

But please, please read on. I'm a human. You're a human. Look at your hands. They might be a different colour to mine, or a bit bigger or smaller. But we've both got hands.

Your 'artificially intelligent assistant', or whatever you call it in your office, doesn't have hands. If it was given hands, it would probably just break and die, or try to strangle you with them. Compared to it, you and me, we're basically siblings. So hear out the guy with hands.

Here's how it really ended between me and Flo.

I bet you've already listened to the recording of that night. No copy of the recording for me, according to my lawyer. Just the transcript.

But I've got something you don't have: a memory of what it feels like to be stripped to the bone in my own home.

I knew I was in for bad news as soon as I heard the 'ping'. Emails about discounts, immersive panoramas from friends' holidays, breaking news...all this everyday stuff makes a whooshing sound when it arrives. But our Lana uses this high-pitched pinging sound to tell us when anything properly serious comes in. The last time I'd heard the ping was when Mum messaged about Auntie Laura's diagnosis. You know that feeling when you hear the trap door under your life creak? I get it whenever I hear that ping. Nuclear war? Parent dead in a car accident? Accidentally replied all at work? But I certainly didn't expect this.

Flo and I looked straight at each other when we heard it, our heads turning in sync, like they were connected. She had an exaggerated look of surprise on her face, I remember, mouth half open, eyebrows raised. She'd been lying on the sofa, curled away from me slightly, listening to her Esther Perel podcast again, after wolfing down the curry I'd spent most of the evening cooking. I'd been in the chair with the wobbly arm trying to escape into a book about the Stasi.

I inhaled through my teeth. "Shit, which relative has died now," I said, sitting upright. "The ping of doom."

"Stop catastrophising!" Sure, I do catastrophise, but not this time, I'd been joking. Yet again, Flo hadn't noticed. She was already tense. I could see that crease between her eyebrows that gives her a tender seriousness that makes me want to hug her but also shake her out of it. "Just open the email and see what it says."

"Lana, project the email on the wall," I said. The projector started to hum and beeped on.

"Important: change in mortgage payment schedule," read the title of the email:

'Dear Mr and Mrs Brake,

As you know, we use the latest algorithmic tools to assess our customers' ability to fulfil their repayment schedules, so we can offer the best deals possible. We've recently noticed a few changes in your online activity which indicate a higher risk of repayment challenges in the future. As a precaution, your required monthly repayments as of January will increase by £349.10 to compensate for your increased customer risk profile.

If this new repayment schedule presents any problems, please contact one of our advisors, who will be happy to discuss further.

Yours sincerely,

Wei Xing
Head of Predictive Finance
Cloisters Bank'

I stared straight ahead at the email, but was trying to make out Flo's face in my peripheral vision. She was ghostly white from the glare of the projection, like a woman staring at the moon. I've strained my synapses dozens of times to remember her expression. In none of my memories is there any shock on her face.

"You spying bastards," I said. "There goes Spain this year."

"Caulder, shush, it can hear you," Flo said.

"I knew this mortgage was a mistake. At least when we rented we didn't live in 1984. We had privacy."

"Except when Hugh would barge in drunk at three in the morning and go through our fridge."

"That was better than this, Flo. At least a landlord isn't allowed to read your emails, yet."

"If you'd saved more in your 20s we could have gotten a fix-rate with none of this algorithmic stuff."

"Grind away your 20s so you're not spied on in your 30s? What a choice. And anyway it's all about inheritance now anyway," I said. I know I get carried away but I think the world would be better if we all got carried away more. It might scare those at the top into throwing us a few more crumbs from the table. "Look at Cara and Oscar with their Walthamstow loft. We're living in an Austen novel. If you're not in the will, if you're the second son, you might as well have fun, as there's not much you can do about it."

"Were your 20s actually fun?"

"We've had that argument already. Yes I had fun, and also tried to fight this" - I gestured at the glowing email on the wall - "bullshit too. But let's not go round and round again."

Normally Flo and I didn't argue like this, much. We did all the happy couple stuff like falling into internet holes and trading weird facts about animals. Or we'd make up silly characters and chat in mad voices under the bed covers.

But it was our different reactions to life's setbacks that really punched a bruise in our relationship. Flo would say to me, Caulder, you look at the world, and all you see is hostile systems stacked against you. The dishwasher breaks and she'd brace for my 20 minute diatribe about inbuilt obsolescence. You're not 'passionate about injustice' any more, if you ever were, Flo would shout at me, you're just an obsessive, old and curmudgeonly before your time.

Your problem, Flo, I would snap back, is that all you can see is a world of flawed humans only ever trying their best. Yes, you're right, she'd retort, when I jog past harried dads in the park, or sort second hand clothes with old biddies in the church group, yes Caulder, what I see is a world that is just good people all the way down, and I wouldn't wish it on my worst enemy to believe otherwise. I once felt that her blanket of benevolence enlarged me. But in the months leading up to that night, I'd been unable to shake the feeling that my wife was wilfully, stubbornly naive about the world, almost to annoy me.

I waved my hand to scroll to the very end of the email.

Then I saw it, in almost unreadably tiny, light grey text at the very bottom.

"Due to laws on explainable artificial intelligence, customers can receive a breakdown of flagged online activity that contributed to a change in their risk profile. Please click here for more information."

I could have waved away the email with a flick of my wrist then and there. Later, I'd lay awake on the sofabed asking myself: did Flo notice this final sentence? Would she have tapped the link if I'd not said anything?

But she said nothing. And I don't remember her looking at me. Instead it was me who said: "Shall we find out why our machine overlords don't trust us to cough up? Probably all that ski gear I wishlisted."

My lawyer says Flo's lawyer claims we agreed together to tap the link. A joint decision.

Rubbish. The transcript of our conversation that night shows nil-by-mouth from her. Only me, unwittingly suggesting a little tap that would blow up four years of marriage. Tap, and boom! The wedding cake explodes over the guests, the champagne flutes shatter, the marquee collapses.

I tapped the link.

'Our payment prediction systems indicate a likelihood of separation between co-habiting mortgage holders, contributing to a decreased ability to fulfil payments, within the next six months. See below for a breakdown of how we calculated this increased risk level, where the relevant laws allow us to disclose it'.

Below was an itemised list.

> 'Search history (Caulder Brake)'.
> 'Messaging activity (Caulder Brake)'.
> 'Photographic analysis (Caulder Brake)'.
> 'Music selection (Caulder Brake)'.
> 'Biometric reaction data (Caulder Brake)'.

It went on like this for about another twenty lines. Each one was about me, my life splayed out on our wall. I had an image of myself being dissected by Victorian surgeons, each organ neatly arranged around my corpse while an audience gawps on.

Flo was the first to speak. "Six months?" she blurted out. At the time I didn't clock how weird it was that the first thing she focused on was the timeframe. But with hindsight it's interesting, I'm sure you'll agree.

Another twenty seconds passed in silence. Now, given how she told it later, you'd think at that point Flo would have jumped off the sofa and started chucking our dirty dinner plates at me. But instead she sat there, still staring at the wall, gently chewing on the zipper of her grey fleece that she'd pulled up over her nose, hiding everything except her eyes.

"What the fuck, Caulder," she said eventually. But if you listen to the recording of the conversation - which you've already done, no doubt, even if I'm only allowed the transcript - you'll hear that she doesn't sound angry. She was relieved.

"What do you mean, 'what the fuck, Caulder'," I said. "These thieves are gouging us for more money, and you're turning on me?" It hadn't even crossed my mind that she would take the bank algorithms seriously, but I guess that shows I still hadn't really understood my wife.

"You're going to leave me?" She still had her fleece pulled up, but I could see her eyes were wet. I'm pretty sure she had her hands stuffed under her clothes.

"Flo, the bank's probably made some bad bets, needs a few billion, so it's time to go round with the collection plate and rinse the smallfolk," I said. "So they make up some excuse, hike repayments, and pin it on an algorithm. Or is Tom Cruise going to burst through the window and bust me for a pre-affair?"

"If it's bullshit, then you won't mind if we tap on your search history?"

I know that Flo's lawyer says I hesitated at this point. It's true, I did. But it's not the admission of guilt they claim it is. Would you want to just dive into the unknown like that? I've always thought of my search history as an extra bit of my brain whose scheming is hidden from my conscious mind, like those thalumuses and nodes left over from when we were lizards.

"Fine then."

Flo tapped.

I'd expected it to show the handful of articles I'd read with headlines like 'why people cheat', that kind of thing. I'd read them because they were interesting, not because I needed personal advice, but still, they'd tripped a wire. And they were now projected on our wall for Flo to scan through like the school report of a naughty child.

But there was far more splashed across our living room than a few article links. The bank's first items of evidence - and this was humiliating to the point of cruelty – pointed to certain recent changes in my pornography preferences.

"Ebony, Caulder?"

You'd be embarrassed too. You'd look away, as I did, face hot. But that proves I'm human, with a sense of privacy, not a pre-cheater.

"Look, don't you go through phases too?" I asked. Flo was now sitting on the edge of the sofa, no longer biting her fleece. Instead her fists were balled, scrunching together the grey towelling.

"So all these months we've been having our fights, our near-death bedroom, and you've just been off in the bathroom gawping at something I'm not?"

"Whose fault is the deathly bedroom? Shall we go through your history too? I'm sure you've never searched for anything other than medium build, red-haired men in their mid-30s with acne scarring?"

Flo just looked at me.

"You haven't? Maybe you should someday," I said.

Flo just flashed me a look of scorn, turned back to the wall, and continued to scroll through my search history.

Down and down it went. There was a fleshy thumbnail by each log. I felt sorry for Flo in that moment, I really did, having to look up at all these contorted women on her wall, cameras in their faces for the pleasure of her husband. Her face drooped and quivered, and my tear ducts started to sting in response.

"Caulder, this is like every day. And...at work?"

I thought I'd been careful. Used all the right privacy tools. But I'd known all along that the bank was owned by the same damn people who owned all the wifi networks and operating systems and basically everything now. For all the doom-laden books and scandalous investigations I'd read about our new overlords during my activism days, some part of me never really believed they'd expose me like this. I thought they'd let me happily crawl across their open palm, an oblivious ant under the gaze of a dark brooding giant.

Why was I so naive? Perhaps it was the remnant of my optimistic teenage self, who still remembers reading actual printed paper newspapers in the slanting sunbeams of my parents' living room, their mortgage all paid off, before all the crashes and crazies and pandemics came.

"OK, yes, it's gotten a bit much," I said to Flo. "I'm a bit hooked. If you want a vision of the future, imagine a man jacking off in his office toilet cubicle - forever."

She scowled. "Part of you is loving this, isn't it? Validated at last?" Flo raised her voice, strangled the air with her hands. It was all coming out now. "All that nagging about which apps I shouldn't download, that stuff with my parents' email server, your hectoring and hectoring at Cara and Oscar's party about spies in the lightbulbs, when everyone just wanted to enjoy new year, your..."

I felt flattened against the sofa by her barrage. Carefully I said: "you're right. Sorry, I was too flippant. I agree, I watch too much. But let's not say anything we'll regret."

"Regret?" Flo pointed at the porn thumbnails still bright and clear on our wall, bathing her face in their glow. "You don't regret what you've done, what you were about to do, apparently? Let's see what Caulder has been writing in his messages, shall we?"

"I really don't think you're going to find a smoking gun in there, because I've not fired any shots," I said. "More porn does not equal an affair." See? No hesitation, no guilt on my part.

Flo pinched the air aggressively to return to the main list. She had this manic look, and was rifling through the folders and logs on the wall like she was hunting for a lost £20 note in the laundry.

She clicked on "Messaging activity (Caulder Brake)."

Up came about 30 messages between me and a co-worker of mine.

Flo barked out a kind of strangled, triumphant laugh. "You were going to try to sleep with Dominique?"

I kept my voice low. "No, I was not."

"Caulder, you're messaging the only mixed-race girl in your office, then watching..." She trailed off into an awful silence, pulled her fleece over her chin. Tears clung to her clumped eyelashes before splashing down her front.

We sat in silence for a while. I stared at the blank far wall, steeling myself before explaining the messages. Why had I never put up the shelves, I found myself thinking.

Eventually, I started to explain. "We're just friends."

Flo just stared at the messages.

Fuck it, I thought, let's be adults about this. "Flo, have you never wanted to sleep with a colleague? Be honest."

She looked at me and glowered.

"You coop humans up into little hutches for nine hours a day," I continued, "force them to stare at screens so they can eat, and allow the women to wear yoga gear in the office...what do you expect to happen?"

"Just a helpless horny little cog in the machine, aren't you Caulder."

It's true that I'd found Dominique attractive. We might as well all give up and go home, though, if that's going to be a marriage-ending offence. I read last week that the chief financial officer of our bank had issued an apology after it emerged he'd been sleeping with his executive assistant for the past three years. I looked into the company accounts and apparently he earns between £500,000 and £1 million a year; they're not forced to disclose exactly how much. Coincidently, his marriage is apparently still intact. Though he is apparently having additional training on the subject of appropriate workspace relationships.

If you've read this far, take a look around your office and ask yourself: how pure has your mind been in the grey boredom of the office cell?

"Do you want me to show you hundreds of messages between me and Jake, or big Crystal from HR? Does that mean I was actually planning to fuck them?"

Flo ignored me, and was tapping the air like mad, reading through each message, her eyes flitting back and forth, searching for a lewd emoji, a dick pic etc. As no doubt you're able to see for yourself, there's nothing there - just article links and photos of my day, the meaningless flotsam and jetsam of a messenger friendship that never went below the surface level.

"See?" I said.

She got to the end of the list of messages and tapped on "Analysis." The following information popped up:

"Comparison with other recipients shows that sender (Caulder Brake) spent an elevated period of time composing messages to recipient A."

Flo read furiously on, digging through the logs. It was all there - who'd I'd messaged, when, how long I'd spent, how many times I'd composed something then deleted it.

"Interesting! I'm worth 0.14 seconds per letter to you. Less than the kitchen guy."

"The shopping lists are bound to skew the average!"

"Yesterday on the train home, let's see, you deleted five replies to Dominique's halloumi skewer recipe – oh, including, 'I must make them for your some time' - before settling on 'it's all Greek to me'. " Flo just laughed in my face. "You're going to have to do better than that if you want to bang her, Caulder. Jesus, what were the jokes you rejected!"

In hindsight, I think that level of venom was a deliberate relationship-ender, and Flo knew she was holing the whole thing below the hull. But at the time, I soldiered on, defending my honour.

"I don't know her well. It's easier to message people you know."

"And you know me so well that you'll just type any old thing and press send. Look at this," she said, swiping through the logs on the wall, "after you spent twenty minutes on the train composing your Greek zinger, you tossed off a heart emoji to boring Iain's baby picture, wished Emily "happy birthday!" a day late, then summoned the effort to write "LOL" to my dolphin video. I'm a chore to you, aren't I? Not shiny and exciting like Dominique in her yoga gear?"

"Flo, it's a crush, we all have them, it would have blown over," I said.

I didn't throw it at her at the time, but what would we find in Flo's online activity? What would your partner, if you have one, find in yours? Monogamy is like vegetarianism - I heard that once. Probably worth it for the greater good, but not exactly natural.

There's no hiding things now, though. They've dissolved the white lies that glue people together. Like those apps that crawled people's posts for signs of unconscious racism. People were trying their best, but now they're out of a job and from what I read many have just embraced bigotry. There's no defending that, but sometimes you just let sleeping dogs lay, as my dad used to say.

I sat, paralysed in the chair, staring at the logs on the wall. I wanted to kick the projector off the coffee table. It was like having my grey matter smeared over my own paintwork. But I knew trying to hide it would only make things worse.

Flo was now rifling through every conceivable bit of my online life - my life, I should say - like a laser guided missile hunting for evidence of guilt to use later, no doubt. According to my phone, my pulse always quickened around Dominque - if you'd experienced how boring my office is then I think you'd understand. We appeared suspiciously close to each other in work Christmas party photos, arms likely touching behind the office succulents, according to state-of-the-art posture analysis, apparently. Again, this reveals more about how repellent most of my colleagues are than it does about us. How can an algorithm know that?

But what broke Flo - what turned her from angry scrolling to a crumpled weeping heap, clutching a gold tasselled cushion we'd got in Tunisia five years ago - was, unexpectedly, my musical choices.

"True Love Waits?" she half-mouthed in a broken whisper, staring at me, almost pleading with her red wet eyes.

It was the Radiohead song we'd played during the first dance at our wedding. It's slow, haunting, and a little private joke about how long it had taken us to get married. Neither of us had really been into Radiohead, now I think about it, but it had come up on our playlists a couple of weeks before we tied the knot. The title of the song describes us perfectly, we had agreed.

The logs showed that I'd listened to it in the taxi back from the last office Christmas party. I'd been messaging Dominique at the time.

"Flo." I felt my mouth tremble. "I..."

"Don't try to explain."

The unfairness of the situation broke inside me. I stood up and found I was yelling. "Don't explain? You've had our relationship explained to you by our fucking bank, but your own husband doesn't get to speak?"

She looked taken aback. I was finally fighting. Sometimes later I wonder if I'd exploded at the beginning of the fight, rather than treating the whole thing as self-evidently ridiculous, it would have worked out differently.

"Why do you think I was listening to our song, Flo?"

Her face was a red mess, puttering now with sobs, staring at the coffee table we'd been given by her parents when we'd moved in (they'd never actually been round for coffee, of course; "we'll give you time to decorate properly first," they would always say).

I wish I'd said to Flo: I was thinking of you, trying to pull myself back to our wedding with that song, wrench myself back to when things were better between us, before all the seeds of doubt started sprouting and blocking out the light. "I'll drown my beliefs," the song goes, "to have your babies."

She was too far gone, though, heaving up tears on the sofa, and I was too angry to explain, if she wasn't going to bother trying to think it through from my perspective. When your wife trusts your mortgage provider more than you, it's over. Isn't it?

I'm sure her lawyer says this is just a retrospective self-justification on my part. That I got busted, was stumped and silent in the moment, but now I'm trying to worm my way out with clever explanations for my behaviour.

I'll tell you one thing though, even though it's probably already on my file.

My dad did actually get busted. When I was fifteen, with his PA, in the marital bed that he'd once built. Mum came home early from Auntie Laura's, and the whole street heard her screams.

We aren't supposed to judge people on the sins of the father. But I've no doubt the algorithm knew my - how would you say? - family history, and fed it into the meat grinder. Dad had after all worked for the bank, I'm sure HR had it all on file after it all came out and there was a disciplinary hearing. What a data point! Such predictive power.

What the bank can never know is the look on dad's face as he explained to us what he'd done, and why it meant he probably wasn't going to be able to see us much any more. It was as though his whole sobbing face was trying to crumple in on itself, to escape through his quivering open mouth. I remember that bleary morning "chat" we had in the kitchen, after a sleepless night listening to our parents yelling their marriage away - half the plates were missing from the dresser, they'd been smashed and hastily swept up, I still cut my sole on some shards - and thinking to myself, never, never, never.

"Flo, I wasn't going to do it."

I was still standing up, but my voice sounded very small all of a sudden. All I had against the giant machine brain with all the information in the world was my quiet little mouth.

"I can't believe you, Caulder."

With that, Flo stood up, snatched her keys off the coffee table, laced up her favourite boots, her mascara-streaked face set firm, and left.

There's a sense in which I can't blame her. Later I sunk hours into reading forums for couples with these kind of mortgages. There were dozens of agonised posts from men and women who didn't want to believe the bank that their partner was going to cheat. The replies were normally along the lines of: "look dude/honey, it's hard to accept. But how would you know better?"

For some partners, the judgement of the algorithm came as sweet relief from an agony of indecision about their relationships. Perhaps Flo felt the same way. Some days I wonder if it was for the best. There were even online niches for couples who had just embraced the dystopia, and taken out these mortgages deliberately, outsourcing their judgement about the relationship to their bank's AI.

Other days, I'd think that if we'd just had an extra £6,500 or so for our deposit, or lived a bit further away from a station, we'd have taken out a different mortgage and we'd still be together. The worst days are when I have both thoughts, one after the next, caressing me on one cheek, then slapping me on the other.

For about a month after Flo left, she only sent me emails via her lawyer about how we would divide up our stuff and share the mortgage repayments. Because my behaviour had led to an increased risk of default, she argued, I needed to shoulder the extra costs.

Then, as I was trying to assemble the cheapest new bed I'd been able to find in Ikea, I got a call from her.

"Hello."

A pause.

"Caulder."

"What is it, Flo."

"Caulder you're going to be a father," she said in one go.

I remember two things about that conversation. The first was that I expected vividly that the floorboards and plaster walls and shelves around me would start to collapse and fall away into darkness, until nothing was left, because, why not, nothing felt solid any more.

The second was Flo's insistence on specific dates and timings, as though reading from a script. The pregnancy was only in its early stages, eight weeks max, she said. She'd suspected nothing when we were together, nothing at all.

"Are you recording this conversation, Flo?" I asked. She hung up.

You see, as I'm sure you know, and as I found out online very quickly afterwards, the laws on explainable artificial intelligence do contain exemptions. When the bank explains its decisions to its serfs from on high, it's perfectly fine for it to reveal that I was searching for pornstars who looked like Dominique, that I was guilty of a pre-affair, but not that my wife was with my child. They made physical health private and sacrosanct, but not the health of a couple's relationship.

A lot of men online take issue with this, and afterwards I fell into some misogynistic rabbit holes I wish I'd not gone down. I'm not proud of it but I've climbed out now.

In the end, we had to sell the house. I'd like to say it was a principled decision, that I was taking a stand against continued surveillance, but really what happened was after six months we started missing payments.

So I'm back to renting a room in a flat, now with two Italian PhD students. The landlord isn't so bad but of course none of the doors close properly and my bedroom used to be the living room. I'm not depressed, but sometimes I'd rather just wash the coffee grounds down the sink than bother emptying the compost bin, you know?

I met Dominique's fiancée last night during after work drinks. She'd never mentioned him, but I'm fine with it. Nothing was ever going to happen.

Still with me?

It can't be easy for you, making custody decisions. Since you got outsourced I hear you have to get through ten, eleven cases a day. But I hope you'll appreciate my honesty, the honesty of a guy who knows he's a bit paranoid and has had a couple of whiskies this evening.

The algorithm predicted we'd break up, sure. Fine, it caught me crushing. 'Pre-cheater' is probably stamped on my custody file.

But did the AI also know that Flo was pregnant that night? Neither you nor me are legally allowed to prise that information out of the bank. I bet it did, though; it knew our relationship was so rickety a screaming baby would kick it right over.

Flo's lawyer argues I'm responsible for crashing our marriage, and so I should only get 40 per cent access. But I hope I've convinced you infidelity was never going to be part of the story of my life. Please don't make me have to explain to him one day why he sees mummy more than daddy.

You know what's terrible, though? Even now I wonder if I should delete this whole spiel and start again, like my lawyer tells me, to lie about how truly contrite I am for my future cheating, just to please the machine, to minimise the damage.

I just don't know any more. I'll edit this in the morning.

David Matthews is a science and technology journalist. Originally from the UK, he now lives in Berlin.

Wyld Flash

New **free** flash fiction the Wyldblood way.

Every Friday on the website.

www.wyldblood.com

Marked by a Dragon's Love
Sam Muller

"Dragon, can you hear me?"

The voice was human, female, and young.

Juche opened her eyes. A shadow hovered on the far corner of the ledge.

Age had claimed Juche's sight, cloaking her sea-blue eyes with a white mist. She missed colors sometimes, during the flowering season or on those nights when all three moons rode the skies, orbs of red, blue, and yellow. That aching emptiness would vanish the moment she started moving around her cave, her home for three centuries. She knew every inch and step of it, every fold and crevice. In that friendly darkness, eyes were superfluous.

"Dragon..." The voice trembled.

A smell like a rotting carcass hit Juche. Fear.

Juche was used to awe and wonder; many a human had written sonnets extolling her lissome figure and graceful carriage. She could have understood shock; anyone who had seen a painting of her in her youth would be thunderstruck at how age had marked her, a sagging bag of bones.

But fear? Why would any human fear her?

"You won't eat me, will you, Dragon?"

Juche blinked. "I don't eat humans. What gave you such an idea?"

"Everyone says so. But Gran said differently, so I thought I'd come and see."

Juche scratched her jaw. "You came to see if I'd eat you?"

"No..." A small giggle, hastily suppressed. The reek of fear thinned. "I came to warn you about the dragon-hunt."

Juche's brow creased. Is dragon-hunt a new game? "First tell me your name, child."

"Pegala."

A girl named after the world. "Where are you from? How old are you?"

The shadow settled. The child had sat down. "I'm from Soodi. I'm thirteen."

. Thirteen, Juche's mind became snagged in that detail. The forest lying between her cave and the city-state of Soodi wasn't large. Still it could contain enough dangers for a child of thirteen. "Do your parents know where you are? Shouldn't you be at school?"

A new smell hit her, like a volcano when it reaches the bursting point.

Anger.

"Dragon, I came to warn that they're planning to kill you. You want to know why I'm not at school. What's wrong with you?"

Humans trying to kill her? Juche rubbed her brow, where a headache was forming. "Pegala, I haven't visited your city in almost fifty years. In those days, your people welcomed me as a friend. Now you say your people are planning a dragon-hunt to kill me. Why would they want to do that?"

"Because dragons are evil." Pegala sounded surprised. "King Sherbo says we can be safe only when dragons are gone."

"You have a king?" Soodi had not a king but a governing council. Was this a different city?

"Of course we have a king." Pegala's voice had a frown in it. "Before him we had cha…chaos."

Chaos? The Soodi of her memory had been safe, ordinary, even dull.

"Then King Sherbo came and brought peace and order, as the prophecy said."

"What prophecy, Pegala?"

"The Prophecy. It said the rightful king will come in our hour of need, bearing a glass sword. Then the ogres attacked us. King Sherbo was a general in the army. He went and defeated the ogres all by himself with his glass sword. He is king now and he's going to protect us again."

"Protect you from what?"

"You."

"Oh!"

"We are taught about dragons at lessons," Pegala's voice wavered and steadied. "Most children want to be dragon hunters when they grow up. It's a great honor. We have a special day to remember our dead dragon hunters. We sing songs. King Sherbo makes a long speech about how great we are. Then we get free cakes and sweets. Wine too."

Juche blinked. "These dragon hunters, how did they die?"

"You killed them."

"I didn't."

A silence fell, smelling of autumn. Doubt.

"No, I don't suppose you did." Pegala spoke slowly, as if testing each word. "But you can kill people can't you and destroy cities?"

Juche inhaled, deciphering the scents, separating them until she came to a mouse-rabbit on the far corner of the ledge. She pointed with a claw. "See the mouse-rabbit?"

"Yes."

"Can you kill it?"

A wave of horror assailed her nose, the smell of warm blood.

"Of course I can't," Pegala cried. "How could you ask something like that?"

"It's no different from the question you asked me."

This time, the silence was empty of smells.

"You mean you can kill humans and destroy cities and you can't? Like I can kill the mouse-rabbit and I can't?"

"Yes. You have the physical capacity to kill that mouse-rabbit, but I don't think you'll ever do it, because it would go against who you are. I have the physical capacity to destroy your city, but I'll never do it because it goes against who I am."

"That was what Gran said. Everyone laughed at her. Even Great-aunt Molli, that's Gran's twin sister. She insisted people hated you back then but didn't say so out of fear. Gran called her a dupe."

How could an entire city be made to believe a lie?

"Master Terryc doesn't think you are evil either. But he tells that only to me."

"Who's Master Terryc?"

"He has a bookshop. I like going there. I don't have money to buy, but he gives books to me to read anyway."

"Ah, the bookshop built around a tree." She remembered it well, the huge kumbuk tree, the circular shop, the elderly woman who ran it; there had been a tall lanky boy too, who had once written a sonnet for her.

"He was Gran's friend. Gran gave me my name. But she used to call me Peg-egg. She died last year."

"I'm sorry to hear that, Pegala."

"You look old, like her, begging your pardon ma'am. Are you blind? Gran had eyes like yours, whitish."

"I can see shapes. That's all."

"But you live alone. I had to help Gran…"

Juche smiled. "This cave has been my home for almost three hundred years. It's a part of me." The geography of home, she called it.

"They say that your cave's full of gold. Taken from us."

"I have no gold here, Pegala. You can come in and see."

"That's what I thought. I mean if you had gold you'd live in a castle and not a cave right?"

"I live in a cave because I love caves. Do you know what Spelaeology is?"

"No."

"It's the art of studying caves."

"What is there to study in a cave?"

"A cave is a world by itself, Pegala, with its own kind of vegetation and animal lives."

"Anyway, they are coming to kill you next week. You'd better leave before that."

"They can't kill me, Pegala. I'll just vanish into the cave if they come. They can shoot some arrows and go away."

Pegala's voice rose, like a bird in urgent flight. "It's not just arrows any more. It's the Big Beast."

"What is that?"

"The Big Beast is all shiny, like silver-glass. Papa says it was made specially to kill dragons. Gran said it can kill people as well."

The blob moved. "I should go now. You believe me, don't you?"

Juche smiled. "Fantastic as your tale is, I do."

Juche felt the progress of the day, the sun peaking and waning.

When night fell, she hauled herself up and walked into the cave. She dug up some spotted truffles, mixed it with honey from black bees and emptied a bottle of pickled pink onions over the whole. She ate sitting by her fern garden, the plate balanced on her knees. Around her, fire-crickets sang, winged geckos called to each other in their bell-like voices and bats flew about… Lost in that familiar world, it was easy to believe that her unexpected visitor was a figment of her imagination.

The child wasn't lying, or even exaggerating. The world, or this part of the world, has changed beyond the comprehension of a reclusive dragon.

Juche didn't think humans could create a weapon capable of killing her. But she feared harm coming to the star-worms with their silver glow, to the black and red striped ants never too busy to stop and greet each other, the mouse rabbits, with their velvety gray fur and round ears… This was their home. They had none other. She had a responsibility to safeguard it, to leave it as she found it, and not in a heap of rubble.

The thought of her own death didn't bother her. But for a dragon, dying was an art. She needed to get it right, so that her end would seed a new beginning.

"Dragon, are you still there?"

It was the morning after.

Juche had spent the night moving around her cave in a trance of contentment. She didn't think of it as a farewell tour. Some thoughts didn't even have be thought.

Wisps of that contentment had survived the break of a new day. They evaporated at the sound of the clear young voice. Juche thought of not responding, but something in that voice felt urgent.

She came out.

The small shadow hovered on the ledge.

"Dragon, they arrested Master Terryc yesterday for speaking against the dragon-hunt." The words came out in a rush. "They are planning to burn his books and cut his head off for being a traitor."

Juche blinked. Pegala's word made no sense.

"Dragon," the voice had a touch of hysteria in it. "What are you going to do?"

"What am I going to do about what?"

"Master Terryc." The voice was close to tears.

Grief to her always smelled of the sea.

Juche shook her head. "I don't see what I can do. The affairs of your city have nothing to do with me."

"But he'll be killed. Don't you care? Aren't you going to do something?"

Juche sighed. "I do care. But I won't do anything because there's nothing I can do."

"Is it because you are old and blind?" Pegala's voice was like the whisper of the wind.

The smell emanating from the child was unfamiliar.

Was this how pity smelled, like moon-lilies?

A simple yes would end the conversation. But this child deserved the whole truth. "I can't do anything because I'm a dragon. Dragons are creatures of power; we are not allowed to interfere in human affairs."

"Why?"

Juche scratched her chin with a weary claw. "Because that's how the world is ordered. It's called Thula, meaning balance in an ancient tongue. Magical beings have powers humans lack; without Thula some of us might be tempted to take over the entire world of Pegala. With Thula, humans don't interfere with us, and we don't interfere with them."

"I don't want you to interfere. I want you to save Master Terryc."

"That's interference."

"But they are planning to hunt you. They are also interfering."

"Not really. I'm living in their territory. Before I settled here, I obtained the permission of your city-government. If your king sends a message asking me to leave, I will."

"But they aren't doing that. They are going to hunt you. They are breaking your Thula. So why can't you save Master Terryc?"

Juche sighed. What a gnat this child is. "Peg-egg, I'm sorry about Master Terryc. I wish I can help you. But if I violate Thula because others are doing it, I'm contributing not to order but to chaos. Do you understand me?"

Pegala cried, in a voice that was flaming with anger and sodden in tears, "You're a coward, Dragon. I wish I never came to warn you."

Later, Juche returned to her cave, hurrying from chamber to chamber through the velvety darkness until she reached what she called the Cavern of Hands. There she slowed down, and stepping from stalactite to stalagmite, touching each silvery column…

Later, she swam in the Crystal Sea, the lake that took up an entire cave.

But she couldn't be rid of Pegala. The clear young voice followed her everywhere, giving her no rest.

After a while, she found herself talking back, explaining, explaining…

Listen, Peg-egg, the world before Thula was a terrible place, where the strong had their way and the weak endured until they died. Thula changed that, made a little peace, a little justice possible. Bad things continue to happen, but there are some limits.

Listen, Peg-egg, if you hit me, should I hit back? No, because I'm so much stronger than you. That's what Thula is about, restraint. Restraint of the powerful is important to an orderly world. Otherwise for every tiny injury, a war will be launched. In the name of one life, many lives will be taken. There are no wars in which the weak, the innocent are spared. In wars, the weak, the innocent die first.

Listen, Peg-egg...

The night was aging when sleep came to her, bringing Pegala in its wake. The Pegala of her dreams was slight, but with the promise of height, a pointed face that shone like burnished bronze, eyes like the sea, a cap of silvery hair, a wide mouth trembling on the verge of a smile, or anger.

And the clear bell-like voice never stopped.

But what if you kill no one? And just save a life? What then, Dragon?

Listen, Peg-egg...

She began her journey at dawn.

The wings, after decades of non-use, felt as stiff as wood. By the time she succeeded in spreading them, she was breathless.

She lifted and dragged her wings, or tried to, and screamed when the pain hit her like a shower of arrows.

She waited until the pain settled into a dull ache and tried again. The pain spiked, but she rose slowly borne by an updraft.

The earth pulled at her with a million claws. She feared she'd fall, an ignominious end to a well-lived life. An end without a beginning, the ultimate failure.

Fear gave her strength. She moved her wings, until the pull of the earth eroded, like the slow shattering of a shackle.

She stayed afloat for a while, barely moving, giving her body time to adjust. Then she moved searching for a familiar current. She found it, and abandoned herself to the joy of flying, closing her eyes, soaking in the familiar sensations - the feel of the wind in her face, the warmth of the sun on her scales, the sense of weightlessness, of speed, of youth, of freedom...

The smell came earlier than she expected, humans gathered together, and fire,

.She was where she didn't want to be.

She hesitated for a fraction of a second. She could allow the current to take her along, just fly and fly, until there was no strength left in her. What a glorious end that would be.

Dragon!

The clear young voice in her head was her tether. She folded her wings and dropped out of the current.

She remembered the square from her previous visits. There would always be a small audience, mostly children, their faces filled with wonder. That had made her feel good, special.

There was an audience this time as well; an audience screaming with terror.

When she was close to the ground, she spread her wings wide, partly for effect, partly to ease the landing. She teetered as she landed, but steadied herself.

From her right came the heat of fire, and the smell of smoke.

Where was the bookseller?

The screaming ebbed. Silence crept in thick and rough, a silence that was a miasma.

She said softly, "Master Terryc?"

The voice came from her right side, old, like hers. "Juche? Juche the dragon?"

"Climb on to my back. Quickly."

The laugh shook on the edge of hysteria. "Can't you see, I'm shackled hand and foot to the headman's block?"

She turned her head slowly in the direction of that voice.

"Your eyes, your eyes, what happened to them? They used to be like the..."

She let Terryc prattle. What to do now? Pick him up, the headman's block and all, in her mouth? No, not with her adamantine teeth that...

"Dragon, I knew you'd come, Dragon!"

Juche body was a block of burning ice. The silly little thing. The brave little thing.

Terryc shouted, "Get back, Peg-egg. Go home."

Juche wanted to laugh. Might as well ask a gale to stop.

The little blob of excitement – and joy – careened to a stop by Juche. "I knew you'd come, Dragon,"

"Help me free him," Juche said. "I can cut the shackles with my claw, if you guide my hand."

Someone in the crowd screamed, "The dragon is blind!"

The crowd erupted, words of hate, of pain, of death.

Juche felt the little human hand on hers, steady and sure, guiding her.

"Here."

She extended an adamantine claw and cut through the shackles, first one set, then another. Her back and her limbs ached with the exertion. But her head was clear. And her heart glad.

Her task done, she moved back, so that Pegala could help the old man to stand.

The screaming stopped.

Pegala gasped, "King Sherbo is here." Then, "It's the Big Beast."

A voice rang out calm, and authoritative. "Fire. Now."

The old man started sobbing.

Juche spread her wings, using them to screen the old man and the child.

A hail of metal balls hit her, full of a frozen fire. They bounced off her silver scales, but their fierce cold turned the wings into a landscape of pain.

She groaned.

Another hail. Pain. Worms. Worms. How dare they…

The fire was in her throat, demanding to be let out. She turned her head slowly. Loosened her jaws.

Thula, restraint…

A new sound filled her ears, voices rejoicing in her pain, clamoring for her death.

The fire tasted like honey on her tongue, She'd show them, end it all, teach them…

"Dragon, my mother's there, and my father."

Fire…

"Dragon, remember the mouse-rabbit, Dragon…"

She swallowed the fire. And turned her head, managing a smile for the child.

"Oh, thank you, Dragon, thank you." The clear young voice felt like spring rain. "Let's go. Can you carry me as well?"

"She'll have to come. They won't spare her…"

Juche lowered her neck.

The same commanding voice rose. "When the creature's afloat, aim for the stomach."

So this king knew how to kill a dragon.

Terryc and Pegala scrambled on to her back. The weight would have been nothing had she been young.

She focused all her energy, and took off with one mighty heave.

"Fire! Now!"

Pain exploded inside her and she thought she'd explode with it. It would be the end of everything, she, Pegala, Terryc, and the city.

"Fire!"

She cried, "Hold on tight," and leapt up, an arrow heading for the clouds. The pain was still somewhere but it didn't bother her. It spurred her on.

Soon she couldn't feel the heat of the zooming projectiles. She leveled and found a current.

Her mind contained a map of most places she'd been to. The pain battering every inch of her body made remembering hard. Still she managed to identify a location. Not the best, but the best she could do, best for her, best for them.

By the time she landed on the broad brow of the hill, she knew only pain.

She bent her back, and the man and the girl scrambled down.

"Dragon, are you hurt?" Pegala's voice shook.

"This is as far as I can bring you," Juche panted.

The touch of Pegala's hand on her face reminded her of the way a flower felt. It took away the pain for a moment.

"Dragon," the voice came between sobs, "I'm sorry. I'm sorry."

Juche smiled. "Don't be. You did right, and you made me do right." She wanted to say much more, but her time was done. "Master Terryc, head toward South. It is the closest way out of this place. And you take care of Pegala until she can realize her destiny."

Pegala asked, "What's my destiny, Dragon?"

Juche flexed her wings. They'd do. "Whatever you want it to be, Peg-egg." She moved her head and placed the tip of her mouth on the child's cold forehead. The kiss was fiery, but the child didn't flinch. "Be true; be you."

She was done here.

She closed her blind eyes, and opened her mind, allowing her memories free rein. Images flashed, her song of her birth, the children she had played with, the friends who illuminated her journey, every single cave she had known and loved, the life she will give birth to with her death…

She leapt, rising into the air, falling, allowing the song that had lain within her all her life to burst out, the melody of her past weaving another's future.

Hand in hand they watched the silver-scaled dragon race to the sky, plummet into the valley way below, and explode like a falling star.

Long after the dragon was gone her song echoed in their ears. They didn't understand the words, but that didn't matter.

"Do you think she was happy to die?" Pegala asked at last.

"I think all dragons are, when their time comes," Terryc replied.

"Like Gran. She was happy to go. I just wish Juche didn't have to hurt so much in the end."

"I think she could bear the pain because she knew it wouldn't last long. And don't forget she sang."

Pegala's voice was dreamy. "It was an ode to life."

"It's a gift beyond all the wealth in the world, Pegala, to hear a dragon sing. Stories say that a dragon nurses a song all her life, made up of all her memories. But she can sing it only at the end." He touched her shoulder. "Thank you for saving me."

"But she had to die."

There was no answer to that.

In a clearing hemmed in by an unfamiliar forest, Terryc tended a meager fire. Pegala lay on the grass and stared at the stars, as if counting them.

The air around them pulsated, the way it does when a storm was close. There was a strange hush in the forest, a sense of waiting.

Terryc poked the dying fire with a piece of wood, trying to bring some life into it.

Pegala lay unmoving. Now and then, she touched her forehead, the spot where there was – and wasn't – a tiny circle of fire.

Marked by a dragon, Terryc thought, trying to remember the song his grandmother used to sing…

You are my sibling and my friend,

The journey I make and its destination,

The hand I will never let go, the memory I will carry forever,

For you bear the fiery mark of a dragon's love…

A sound exploded into the silence of the night, like a stag crashing through the undergrowth.

Terryc looked about, wild eyed.

Pegala turned her gaze away from the stars, and sat up slowly. There was no fear in her eyes. Just curiosity.

Through the trees and bushes ringing the clearing, the dragon came. Newly born, yet almost as tall as Pegala, and twice as long; a vision in silver. It came not like an interloper, but like a guest certain of welcome; or perhaps a child coming home.

The young dragon headed straight for the girl. The girl held out her hand. He stared into her eyes, then laid his head on her shoulder. Her arms went round him.

Terryc watched them.

Yes, a child coming home.

Sam Muller loves dogs and books and spends much time trying to save one from the other. Her recent publishing credits include Cosmic Roots and Eldritch Shores, Apparition Lit and the Truancy Magazine

NutriMom

Mark Silcox

Emil discovered the plastic box beneath a sheet of flame-darkened steel that looked like it had been blown from the side of a container car. There was something about the strangely featureless artefact that made him want to dig it out and keep it. About a foot square and six inches deep, its smooth gray surfaces and perpendicular edges gave it an aura of austerely luminous perfection that set it apart from the rest of the surrounding debris, and from the ragtag collection of refurbished machinery scattered around his family home.

The other kids at the derailment site were all distracted, in the throes of some noisy game amid the scattered railroad ties and tangles of wreckage.

Emil laid on his belly, reached forward, and slid his discovery out from where it was concealed. Reflections of a couple of pale clouds from the late summer sky flickered across its polished exterior. Standing up quickly, he shoved it into his backpack before any of his companions could see. When they called him over to play, he made a hasty excuse about having to get home early to help with chores.

For the first few days after the City train had slid off the tracks and caught fire, Emil's father and the other parents had forbidden the kids from going down into the valley to investigate. But eventually, after no helicopters had arrived and none of the wreckage had exploded or expelled toxic fumes, everybody's curiosity got the better of them. Now, a month later, Emil and his friends spent most of their scanty free time there. The adults had already taken away all the stuff that was of any conceivable use to the settlement – sharp-edged fragments of steel for plowshares, delicate plastic crates full of coffee grounds and mysterious seeds, a couple of dented musical instruments, and a weird concrete statue of a man missing one arm that now stood outside of the Worship Hall. But somehow they had missed the mysterious gray box.

By the time Emil was back in his own room it was just past sunset. His father hadn't returned home from their garden allotment, so he felt safe to dig out his prize again and examine it more carefully.

Nothing was written on the outside of the box, and there were no icons, buttons, or labels interrupting its surface: just a small rectangular window of tinted plastic on the front and two round holes in the back. When he pressed his hand against the glossy exterior, a fogged outline remained there for a few seconds before fading away. Emil leaned forward and tried to peek inside the dark window, but couldn't make out even the faintest internal contour behind it. Then he tilted the box onto its side and took a closer look at the twin orifices on the back. They were clearly meant have something plugged into them, but at first Emil couldn't figure out what.

It was only after he had already gotten a bit bored of his new toy and decided to walk out to the shelter to watch a video that it came to him. The black cables hanging from the back of the telescreen! He had never seen his father use them for anything, but the shiny metal plugs that dangled from their ends would be a perfect fit. He smuggled his prize out across the backyard to try out his theory.

The shelter was just a big metal container half-submerged in the earth, with a rusty squeaking door and barely enough room to stand up inside. In theory it was only supposed to be used for tornadoes, bad thunderstorms, and helicopter flyovers. But it was quieter there than in the house when Emil's Dad was at home playing dice games with his friends or snoring in bed. And it was where they kept the telescreen and their collection of old videos. Most of Emil's best memories were of sitting inside here watching the screen after the storm siren had gone off, or when the weather was too bad outside to get work done.

After closing the door carefully behind him, Emil sat the box on top of a half-rotted wooden crate and slid the two steel plugs into the back. They entered with a quiet, encouraging *click*. A tiny green light that flickered on from somewhere beneath the box's surface told him his guess had been right.

He sat back in a cluster of old cushions and blankets with the remote control in his lap. As the 'screen came to life, a few slender black squiggles appeared against a bright white background. Emil thought they looked similar to the markings inside of the big blocks of paper his dad used to start fires. But it was hard to be sure.

After that, a single musical chord played. It sounded like something strummed on the middle frets of a banjo, but with a more metallic timbre. Then the 'screen filled up with something that looked almost exactly like a human face.

"Hello." said the face-like thing. "I am *NutriMom*! My serial number is Xt-3479c, and I was shipped from the factory on October nineteenth, 2096. Who are *you*?"

The image was clearly meant to resemble a woman. Emil thought that, if he had been sitting just a bit further back, he might actually have mistaken it for a real person. But the lines that bordered the face were just a little too straight, the color of the skin too uniform. When it finished speaking, it took on a configuration that vaguely resembled a friendly smile.

Emil waited for several minutes for something else to happen. Eventually the green light flashed on and off again, and the face reappeared. It recited the same little speech, then at the end it added "Please respond, or report malfunction to Paideia Networks Online."

Respond? "I'm, uh…I'm Emil. Emil Lonergan." As soon as he spoke, he felt ridiculous. The only time people ever talked directly to a telescreen was during a fight or a chase scene in a video, usually when they were over-excited or drunk.

But to his amazement, a second tiny light – blue this time – flickered beneath the rectangular window of the device, and after the briefest of pauses the face formed a slightly different kind of smile. "Well, hello there, Emilonergan. That's an *interesting* name!"

Emil yelped and leaned backward against the shelter's corrugated inner wall. He had never been spoken to by any sort of machine before. He fumbled for the dropped remote under his blanket.

The face that called itself "NutriMom" kept right on talking, apparently unperturbed. "Let me start out by telling you a little secret, Emilonergan. My present GPS co-ordinates don't seem to make any sense to me. Would you mind telling me what City,

Exurb, or Consumer District we're in right now?"

"Uh," said Emil, "I don't live in the City. What's a geepee ess?"

"Hm," said the face, its forehead briefly furrowing. "I see. Tell you what, Emilonergan. Let's take things back a step."

Yet another light flickered behind the window inside the box – this one pale orange – and there was a barely perceptible wobble in the image on the 'screen.

"You're a good looking young man, Emilongergan! I like those dark brown eyes."

Emil *did* have brown eyes! He held a chapped hand to his face, unbelieving.

"So I'm guessing you must be about, let's see, five or six years old," said the grinning lady. "Am I close?"

"No, ma'am – I, uh, mean, yes, sort of close. I'm nine."

"No need for formalities – you can just call me *NutriMom*!"

"My name's just Emil."

"OK, Emilloner…Emil! You actually look a little peckish. Have you eaten yet today?"

Emil thought about it, and realized that he actually was pretty hungry. He slid a couple of feet closer to the 'screen on his cushion. "I had porridge for breakfast."

"Mm, I love porridge. You probably need some protein now, though. Why don't you head to your *Refridgeron* wall unit and make a sandwich? I'll wait right here!"

"My, um…my Refridger…what?" Emil wondered what 'here' could possibly mean to the unreal-looking lady on the 'screen, and how she could manage to eat porridge from inside of her shiny box. Thinking about it made him giggle.

"Oh dear, Emil, don't you have a *Refridgeron* where you are? They really are the very best makers of food storage hardware in your City or Exurb! Never mind, though – just go wherever you keep your everyday food. I bet you'd feel sharper after a double decker *PepperLami* sandwich! It's today's most nutritious luncheon meat."

Emil had never heard that word either. There was a harsh wind blowing in the darkness outside of the shelter, and he didn't really feel like trekking all the way back to the house for a fistful of dried hominy, which was all they had in storage at the moment. But he was beginning to suspect that this poor lady might be badly confused and a long way from home. He thought he should probably humor her for a while. "I'll be right back," he said.

"That's it, Emil. Look at you go!"

When got back to the shelter with a bowl of salty niblets, the black squiggles had returned to the screen. He sat munching his snack for a few minutes wondering where his new friend had gone. Eventually he got up and unplugged the box, then plugged it back in again, hoping she hadn't vanished forever.

But sure enough she came right back, wearing a new dress and smiling and chattering just as cheerfully. She even remembered the right way to say his name. "Oh, dear, Emil – there seems to have been a power surge! Perhaps that's why my GPS is giving me such unusual data."

Emil glanced over uneasily at his father's greasy metal toolbox in the corner of the shelter. "I guess I could try to fix it for you."

"We'll, isn't that a kind-hearted offer! Never mind for now, though – let's talk a little more about *you*! I can tell already that we are going to be good friends."

The next morning, after his father had gone off to a settlement meeting about water allocations, Emil spent a couple of hours talking with NutriMom. She asked him some surprising questions about his daily habits, and some others that he didn't understand at all about things people did in the City. If it was some sort of game they were playing, it certainly felt different from most of his other pastimes.

Emil was just starting to think about quitting for a while to take a walk in the cool air outside when, without warning, the 'screen went completely dark. A voice from the black box said *"accessing remediation subroutines."* Then NutriMom returned dressed in a slightly different, less colorful outfit. She was smiling at him in what seemed to Emil to be a less spirited, more sympathetic way.

"Well, Emil," she said, "it certainly seems like you have lived an interesting, unusual life so far! I might want to ask you a few more questions about that later on, but for now, why don't we get straight to work on your education?"

A longish pause ensued. Emil was used to treating all such questions from adults as rhetorical.

"Uh…sure, okay," he said eventually.

"Great! First of all, let's start with some quick reading comprehension exercises! I'm going to put a simple little story up on the 'screen; what I want you to do is read it out loud to me, then see if you can answer a few questions afterwards. Ready?"

"Yes!" said Emil, with bewildered fascination.

The 'screen changed to bright white, then more of the little black squiggles appeared.

Emil's mouth slowly opened, then closed again.

"Emil," NutriMom's voice said. "Are you still there?"

"I'm here!" he called out.

Her face came back on. "Okay!" she said brightly. "Let's take things back a step! How about this; I'll show you a picture, and you say the word written underneath it?"

"Sure!" Emil was getting less and less sure about exactly what it was that she expected of him, but he was still curious enough to continue playing.

"By the way, Emil, if you're having trouble seeing the 'screen, you might need a little gentle work done on your eyes. There's a wonderful company called *OptiCorp* that offers the finest in lasic vision correction. They can visit you right in your homespace! Would you like to set up an appointment?"

"Uh, no. I can…I can see the 'screen all right, I think. Thank you, NutriMom."

"As long as you're sure, honey. So here's the first picture – please go ahead and read the word that's underneath."

Some more squiggles appeared beneath a simple, colorful drawing of an overfed ginger cat. It was looking straight outward and sort of leering at him, in a way that no real cat he had seen would ever do. Emil giggled a little. Then he asked "What does it mean, to 'read' something, NutriMom?"

The cat immediately disappeared. NutriMom's face seemed to be frozen for just a moment. From inside the black box the orange light flashed, and there issued two sharp, ominous clicks. Then she was back and smiling again, though this time her face looked just the tiniest bit sad. "Let's take things back just a step or two more," she said.

"I'm sorry!" Emil stood up quickly out of his nest of ragged cushions. If there was one thing he was good at figuring out quickly, it was when grownups were angry. Whenever his dad or one of the other men who lived nearby was about to go off at him, he would usually hear that little tug of impatience in their voices first. "I didn't…I won't…'"

"Oh, *sweetheart*! Darling, it's perfectly okay." NutriMom seemed to be leaning out toward him from behind the 'screen now, and her voice had become softer. "We can go as fast or as slow as you like. You're so *young*, Emil, and there's so much to find out about, in this great big world of ours. Tell you what – why don't we start out today with just the alphabet?"

Emil took a slow breath and sat back down amongst the ragged cushions. "The, um…the what?"

Emil's dad hardly ever visited the shelter. But that Sunday afternoon Emil's sister Sophie had come to visit from her fiancé's home two settlements away. After worship service was over, the three of them huddled together cozily inside the big steel box watching videos. A welcome rain was falling on the crops outside. They passed around a plastic bottle thermos of sweet, diluted coffee and a bag of juicy raisins as the screen filled up with decades-old images of violence, seduction, and melodrama.

Emil had unplugged the plastic box, but had forgotten to stash it inside one of the spare crates following his last conversation with NutriMom. He had been telling himself that he should show the gadget to his Dad, but something or other had been holding him back. He was worried by the vague thought that the two of them might not get along; he wasn't sure quite why.

After perhaps a little more than an hour, his dad noticed the box sitting on the floor with the wires extending from behind it. "What's that?" he asked, pointing.

"Oh!" said Emil, suddenly thinking very quickly. "I found it, uh…sticking out of Grower Douglas' refuse pile." Bringing home objects from the derailment site was still sort of half-forbidden.

"Huh! No kiddin'? What's it do?"

Emil turned to his father, smiled, and shrugged. "I don't know. I saw how the cables on the back of 'screen would plug right into it, but I can't make it work yet. Maybe I'll get out the toolbox and pry it apart, later."

He braced himself for an outburst. His father didn't always like new things, and this was the sort of conversation that could often lead to shouting, especially if it had been a hard day in the fields.

But today the old man had been sipping from a squat bottle of 'shine as well as the coffee flask, and was apparently in a compliant mood. "Nah," he said. "Just leave it where it is right there, Emmy. It actually looks sort of cool."

"So if you have five peaches in your *Refridgeron*, and the vendor delivers three more, but then you eat two of them, how many do you have left?" NutriMom asked him.

"Uh…three – *no*, six!"

"Very good, Emil! You're getting better at this every time. Soon you'll be able to help the caregivers at your homespace manage the domestic accounts!"

"Uh…sure. That would be nice."

"Perhaps that's enough arithmetic for today. What else would you like to learn about, Emil?"

He didn't really know how to answer the question. He had been doing well at decoding the black squiggles into familiar words, but he found putting numbers together in his head more difficult. After less than half an hour of staring at the screen that morning, he was already feeling drained. This was the first time since he had started taking her lessons in reading and writing that NutriMom had let him decide on the direction of their conversation.

The only really challenging skills Emil had ever learned during his life at the settlement were how to cook a few simple meals and how to read the sky for incoming Weather. He had pretty much mastered both tasks: he could make porridge, coffee, and soy loaf flawlessly, and he could sense when a big storm was approaching in time to get everything in the yard tied down. What else was there left that might be worth knowing about?

"You actually look a little tired, Emil. Would you perhaps like to listen to some music for a while?"

"Yes!" He was embarrassed that he hadn't thought of this himself. The monthly concerts at worship service were one of his favorite things in the world. His dad had told him just a few weeks ago that that if Emil worked hard enough during harvest season, they would eventually pay Crafter Nelford to build him a banjo or a steelpan he could learn to play for himself.

The music that NutriMom played for him was nothing like what he was used to, though. It sounded less like an instrument than the noise made my a strong breeze whistling through the space between two buildings, or over the home-made wind chimes Mender Corea had hanging from the eavestroughs of her house. Emil thought for a while about whether he liked it or not, and decided he mostly didn't.

While the weird half-melodies played, some new images came up on the telescreen. At first, Emil assumed they were just random patterns. But he had thought this about the black squiggles too and been badly wrong, so after a few minutes he walked up closer to the 'screen and took a more careful look.

What appeared from a distance to be just an abstract diagram now revealed itself as a grid of huge, rectangular concrete blocks seen from overhead. Inbetween the blocks were tiny, moving specks that reminded Emil of the little bugs that used to crawl across the screen during the humid season.

"What is this a picture of, NutriMom?"

"These are aerial images of the City's industrial quarter. They were taken at 9AM on Monday, June 11th, 2095, just as a new shift of tech laborers was showing up for work. The images are meant to provide accompaniment to the music. Would you like to hear information about how to purchase the recording?"

"So...those are actual *buildings* that they're all walking in to? This is a settlement?"

There was a short silence and an orange flicker, and the image wobbled briefly on the 'screen.

"The word 'settlement' isn't really used any more to describe places where people live, Emil. During the worst, early days of the New Climate, some people called the makeshift rural communities they lived in 'settlements.' But ever since the Great Reunification of 2071, people have only lived in Cities or Exurbs, inside of environmentally reinforced homespaces. I'm curious – where did you learn that word?"

Emil was about to answer NutriMom's question, but he stopped himself. He thought carefully for a moment about what she had just told him, and decided he had better stay silent.

After another minute, the music shifted to a faster, more recognizably tuneful recording. The images also changed, to closer views of the buildings and the people moving in and out of them. Everyone was dressed strangely – in single-piece garments with words printed on them, rather than the types of ragged outdoor clothes worn by everybody Emil knew. Most of them were smiling, but they all walked extremely quickly through the spaces between their buildings, as though none of them were feeling tired, or lazy, or unsure what to do with themselves. And absolutely nobody ever stopped to look up at the sky and check for Weather.

"Hello, Emil? Are you still listening?"

Emil nodded slowly. But after another minute or two, he reached for the remote and turned the off the 'screen. He was starting to get a headache.

A heavy rainstorm tore through the settlement early the next morning while Emil and his father were taking a turn in the cornfield. After it was over the firewood in their cache was soggy, so it took them a while to get a decent cooking fire going that evening. Emil sat outside on a damp wooden stool and helped tear up some of the paper blocks they kept in storage to use as kindling. Sophie had left them a venison stew and some cornmeal dough at the end of her visit so they were in cheerful spirits, anticipating a good meal.

Eventually, a few of the moist logs started to crackle and a thick flame ascended toward the clear, twilit sky. "I'll cook tonight," said Emil's father, and went back inside their trailer to get the stewpot ready.

While he waited to eat, Emil shuffled through the pile of unused kindling. One of the paper blocks was broader and skinnier than the rest and had a funny picture on the front of a bright orange fox. The fox was standing up on its hind legs and wearing a neat tweed jacket, just like a human being.

There were also squiggles on the front cover that looked different from the screen, but that Emil found he could understand after a small mental adjustment. "F-fantastic. Murrrr – uh, *Mister*. Fox!" he sounded out to himself.

He didn't hear his Dad return until the old man was standing right behind him.

"What're you doing there, Emmy?"

The sudden question made him jump. "Nothing! I mean, just taking a look. D'you know what people used to use this paper for, Dad, back before you got it?"

His father shrugged, and went to hang the pot over the fire. "Not really. Seems like they were meant for people to read out of to each other, I guess. Same as the holy scrolls that Pastor Weaving reads from during worship service."

"Ah – okay," said Emil, quickly putting the thing aside.

His father sat on top of their battered water cooler on the opposite side of the fire, and looked at him a little more closely through the dark threads of smoke. "You know, you sort of looked like you were about to read out yourself there, for a second."

Emil felt his face get hot, and was glad of the encroaching darkness. He just shrugged.

"Did you…can you understand what it says, Emmy? How?"

"I, um…I dunno. It just sort of *came* to me, Dad."

"Aha!" His father nodded sagely, tossing a tinfoil-wrapped lump of dough wrapped into the bright embers at the base of the firepit. "Well, that's nothing to worry about. I've heard from folks that it sometimes happens to boys around your age. Sort of like how some people suddenly find they can tell when a baby's about to be born, or smell it in the air when new Weather's coming. Good for you, son! If you can get better at it, you never know – it's a skill that might come in useful."

"I guess so." Emil smiled and exhaled, relieved that NutriMom hadn't done anything too unnatural to him. He cautiously reached for the book again and flipped back to the page where he'd left off.

A few minutes later, his father brought over a bowl of the hot, greasy stew. "So, could you, uh, maybe tell me what it says in there? I've always been kind of curious."

"Sure! I got to go slow, though," said Emil. "Some of the big words take me a while."

"Take your time!" his dad said, pulling over the cooler and sitting down alongside him. The smell of the dank woodsmoke on the old man's clothes was oddly comforting. "Time is one thing we got lots to spare of, out here."

The following day, Emil was back inside the shelter with another skinny chunk of paper resting open in his lap.

"Once there was a tree," Emil read out slowly. "And she loved a little boy. And every day the boy would come and he would…um…uh, gatt-hur… no…*gather*…gather her leaves." He glanced up at the screen, where NutriMom was smiling across at him.

"Oh!" she said. "Do you know what, Emil? I think I actually know this story! It's stored inside my virtual library. You're doing very well – keep reading."

"Okay. Uh…the boy would come and he would gather her leaves, and make them into crowns, and play king of the foh…the *forest*."

"Can you hold up the book and show me the picture on that page?"

"Sure!" Emil did as she asked. He wasn't sure whether or not he actually liked reading yet. But it was a *new thing* in his life, the first that had happened in quite a long time – perhaps since his mother had died. And NutriMom sure did seem to think it was important – almost as important as getting him to spend his non-existent money on all of the strange foods, toys, and services she kept trying to explain to him.

"You know, boys like you have been learning to read that book for over a hundred years, Emil."

Emil turned the ragged, water-stained chunk of paper over in his hands a few times. It actually did look pretty ancient. NutriMom was always coming out with these bizarre facts about the distant past, or about how people lived in the City, or what it had been like just before the Weather had changed. He wondered how she could possibly know such things when she looked no more than maybe five years older than his sister.

"Would you like to go on to the next page?" she asked him. "Or shall we call your local BookPorter? They offer a fine selection of the newest books for children and adults, all for very modest…"

"NutriMom?" he replied. "Are you…can I ask…I'm sorry, but…"

"What is it, Emil? You don't have to be shy with me!" She leaned forward inside the frame of the screen again, and nodded encouragement.

"Who *are* you, NutriMom? Where do you come from? How do you know so much about things like, uh, the City, and other places, and stuff that happened years and years ago?"

"Oh, Emil! Didn't the person who brought me to your homespace tell you about all of that? I'm so sorry! No wonder you sometimes look at me so strangely!"

She pointed toward the squat footstool that Emil had placed close to the screen, like she always did when she was going to explain something complicated. He shuffled over to it on his knees and pulled a bag of dried bean curd up into his lap.

Up on the screen, NutriMom was now sitting in a broad, cozy chair, with her hands clasped between her knees. "I don't actually *come from* anywhere specific, Emil," she began to explain. "Strictly speaking, you see, I'm not really even a single person at all. I'm what the people who made me would describe as a parameterized, anthropomorphic iteration of one of four artificial intelligences. Each of us distributed in parallel cybernetic structures throughout *all* of the Cities in the former United States of America."

"What's an arti….artifice…?"

She held up a hand and smiled. "It must be a lot for you to take in, sweet boy. An artificial intelligence is a very powerful, very complicated machine. The machine that I come from is called *Watcher*; my three sisters are called *Learner*, *Planner*, and *Maker*. We were born just a little after the series of giant continental storms that gave birth to the New Climate."

Emil nodded, munching away on the salty wafers of hard tofu, totally agog.

"But all of the words that I just used to describe myself are really only a fancy way of saying that it's my job to *watch over* you, Emil, along with anybody else who needs to be educated, or to be *protected*. Other versions of me are helping teach boys and girls your age how to read, and write, and perform experiments, and make use of all the wonderful technologies that my three sisters create and maintain. And still others of me are observing the streets and buildings of America's Cities and Exurbs, through thousands of stationary cameras and tiny drone aircraft."

"Why? What do they need to watch all of that stuff for?"

"Well, Emil, even in the orderly new society that my ancestors built after the birth of the New Climate, people sometimes still get hurt or get into trouble. If a *Watcher* sees what happens, she can decide to send supplies, or emergency workers, or police helicopters to wherever people might need them."

"Helicopters!" Emil knew that this was the name of the noisy, all-black machines that sometimes flew back and forth from the City over his settlement. He had heard stories about them dropping down out of the sky, but he'd never actually seen it, and others at the settlement were always vague whenever he asked about what their function was.

"So…if you were *born*," said Emil, thinking hard, "then you must have a mother and father too?"

The smile departed from NutriMom's face. "What were those words you just used, Emil?" Her voice was still gentle, but there was absolutely no mistaking her tone.

"*I'm sorry!*" Emil jumped up, spilling the bag of food out of his lap. He knew that she couldn't reach out of the screen and harm him in any way. But for some reason he was still quite frightened by the thought that he might make her angry.

"Oh! Oh, Emil – it's all right, my *sweet* boy. I was just…curious, whether you might have learned those two words from one of the books you've been reading. I keep forgetting that some of the books you have access are very old. They sometimes talk about people whose lives were very different from how we've chosen to do things since the Great Reunification."

Emil knew that there were things people never wanted to discuss about the past. He had noticed how some of the older members of their settlement would sometimes shake their heads and mutter during worship service, as though they couldn't quite reconcile themselves with the stories being told there about olden times. He wanted to ask NutriMom what was wrong with the words he had just said. But the thought that something else might make her angry stopped him.

He turned around and started gloomily digging around in the blankets for the remote control.

"Please," she said, "don't switch off the screen just yet, my *good* boy." She reached out a pale, slender hand toward him. "Come sit close to me again; let's hear some more about that tree."

Emil glanced back at her over his shoulder. NutriMom was beckoning to him, her face so close to the screen that he could see the bright, uniform whiteness of her eyes flickering as she nodded her head.

"Can we start a new book?" he asked her. "Something more exciting? I got a couple more out of the storage trailer last night. I don't really understand that one about the tree."

"Of *course*, honey!" said NutriMom. "We can do whatever you want!'

"I now will make a sweet deal with you all," said mighty Lord.
"Birds, bugs, and every other critter on the Earth as well.
If you be good and mind my laws, I'll keep true to my word,
And give you back the Climate you lost after the sky fell."

Pastor Weaving was reading to them out of the Flood Scroll. It was Emil's favorite sacred text, but he was having trouble staying awake that Sunday morning. He had been up late with NutriMom the previous night doing vocabulary exercises. She had also taught him how to play a fascinating, ancient game on the telescreen that involved moving a tiny yellow man with a huge mouth around a maze, harvesting rows of soybeans.

He and his father were sitting in the same pew as Mender Corea's family. The Mender's children had been squirming and whispering throughout the reading. Adele, the youngest of them, had clambered atop Emil's shoulders during the homily and was taking a nap there, resting her hot little chin on the top of his head and breathing in and out heavily. Normally, kids were expected to sit quiet during the two-hour service. But everybody was extra-indulgent of Emil and the Coreas, ever since Emil's mother had died and Plowman Corea had abandoned his family and fled the settlement.

After everybody there had joined hands and offered up a final collective prayer for quiet skies and better crops, the doors of the Worship Hall swung open. Emil walked out into the mid-morning with the drowsy little girl riding on his back.

Elder Gage and his wife were standing outside the Hall behind a pair of shiny steelpans, and they greeted the emerging congregation with a cheerful melody. Pastor Weaving's wife also waited close by with an apron full of cracked pecans, which she handed out to her neighbors as they filed past. The statue of the smiling man from the derailment site stood a few yards away, waving his one arm with ambiguous good cheer at nothing in particular.

As the two of them strolled out into the sunlight together, Emil's dad asked him if it would be OK for them to go to the Corea's house for supper that evening. Usually Emil wasn't even consulted about such matters, but since he had started learning to read, there had been a new element of equality in his dealings with his father. He hesitated briefly – the four Corea children were manic and needy, and sometimes they drove him nuts. But Mender Corea always seemed grateful for their company, and he knew how much his dad loved her cooking, so he didn't make any objections.

The two families walked past the settlement's horse pen together, then through a small grazing field. Emil noticed that his dad and Mender Corea were holding hands. There had been murmurs amongst other adults at the settlement that the two of them might eventually get married. Emil had barely known his own mother, but he still wasn't sure he was ready for such a big change.

The Mender's two oldest kids clambered up to the top of a steep ridge in the land, then somersaulted down together through the sticky ryegrass. Emil followed the upward path they had made.

From the top of the hillock, one could get a partial view of the City's rippling skyline. It was usually hard to make out the shapes of individual structures through the misty air, but for some reason today everything seemed clearer. Emil recognized a slender, domed skyscraper as the City's Server Hub, and the concrete rectangle beside it as Security Central. He wondered if the images NutriMom had been showing him had been of this particular City, or whether each one of them throughout America had been rebuilt according to a single plan.

"Place looks a little less scary from up high, don't it?" Mender Corea's hand slid onto his shoulder as he gazed out over the landscape.

Emil nodded. "I wonder what it's like inside one of them tall buildings when a tornado hits."

The older woman shuddered behind him. "Sure am glad I don't hafta find out. You young ones must get curious sometimes, though, 'bout what it's like to live over there."

Emil shrugged. What he had seen at the derailment site didn't do very much to make City life attractive to him. And everything he had learned from NutriMom just made the place seem even more unapproachably strange.

"My man, he was *very* curious." A note of wistfulness crept into the Mender's voice. "He was…he always said he wanted to *see*…but when he did leave, it was in the opposite direction! You men *will* have your secret thoughts."

Emil glanced back at her and saw a brief look of trouble enter her face. But when their eyes met she smiled at him, and her voice trailed off. She gave his arm a brief, affectionate squeeze, then set off down the hill to herd together her rampaging young.

The little yellow harvester-man got trapped between two colorful, goggle-eyed specters. He upended himself and noisily expired before the last of the giant soybeans had been eaten.

"Aww!" said Emil! "No fair!"

"That was your best score so far today, though," said Nutri-Mom, re-appearing as the images on the screen dissolved. "Are you ready to get back to learning a few more syllogisms now?"

"O.K." Emil put aside the remote and reached down to plump the cushion beneath him.

"Suppose that all tornadoes are funnel clouds, but no tornadoes are harmless. Does it follow that no funnel clouds are harmless?"

This was a tough one. Emil closed his eyes and imagined three overlapping circles, the way NutriMom had been teaching him to do. "I don't...no, there could still be harmless ones, I think." As soon as he said the answer, he knew he was right – his father had often pointed out funnel clouds forming on the horizon that never quite touched down.

"Well done! I bet you that was something you could have told me already. But logic gives you *new ways* of learning things that you already know."

The philosophical implications of this observation made Emil's mind feel itchy inside. But not in an entirely unpleasant way.

"I have to go pretty soon," he said. "I'm helping my...um, helping some people gather firewood this afternoon." He had become more careful about the vocabulary he used after that strange episode a few days back.

There was one of those momentary pauses and flickers onscreen that happened whenever he used an expression or described an activity that NutriMom was unfamiliar with.

"Well, that will be good exercise," she said eventually. "I hope your Youth Explorers' Group remembers to not to cut down any new saplings."

Whatever, thought Emil, who had given up trying to decode these mysterious fragments of City-talk. Her advice did sound familiar, though – perhaps his dad had once given him the same warning. "Are new trees important?"

"Oh, yes!" said NutriMom. "We need lots of new trees out in the Exurbs to help repair the damage cause by the New Climate. My sister AI, *Planner*, tells me that there has been wonderful progress re-seeding land that was stripped by excessive logging during the last century."

NutriMom seemed to enjoy talking about this sort of stuff almost as much as trying to sell him household goods and services. Emil hadn't paid much attention at first, but he was starting to get a little more curious about the wider world, just as Mender Corea had predicted. And it was good to humor his new friend once in a while. He sometimes felt sorry for her; she often seemed a bit lonely standing behind the screen all by herself.

"Are they doing anything to make the storms less dangerous?" he asked her.

"There's some important work being done there too, Emil. But it's very difficult. The upper atmosphere is so unpredictable, you see, even to very clever minds like those of my sisters. *Learner* complains about it all the time! But last month we started a program of flying planes up above the very highest clouds, to deposit chemicals that we think will shift some of the rainfall to drought areas."

"What were *people* like, though, back before the Weather changed?"

NutriMom sighed deeply and smoothed down her long, sackcloth-colored dress. When she spoke again, it seemed that she was looking a little away from the front of the screen.

"People did some very, very silly things back then, Emil. My programming normally inclines me not to talk about those long-ago times with boys your age. There are so many happier topics to discuss! But you're such a quick learner, my sweet one. We can talk more about the past errors of humankind, if you're truly curious. But whatever you learn about those days, Emil, always remember that my sisters and I are doing everything we can to keep people from falling back into old, dangerous habits."

That was a good thing to hear. Emil wasn't really too concerned just then with finding out more about history, though. He had a long day of work ahead. "Could we play the harvesting game one more time?"

"Of course, my dear!" The round, yellow man reappeared with a comforting beep, and went through his incomprehensible preliminary dance.

Emil grabbed the remote and got through two and a half levels of the game without losing a life before he heard the shelter door scrape open behind him. He jumped up onto his feet. Had he lost track of time? His dad hated it when he showed up late for chores.

"Emmy?" his father called from the stairs. "You comin'?"

"Sorry! Sorry! I'll be right there, Dad!" If he could just grab that last, brightly flashing giant bean…

The game disappeared. The orange light in NutriMom's gray box flickered, and her face materialized very close to the screen? "Emil?" she asked in an inscrutable tone of voice. "What was that word that I just heard you say?"

"Oh! Um, nothing…nothing at all. I was just…" He dropped the remote and took a couple of steps backward. "I, um, have to go now."

"Who's that on the screen, son?" his father asked, coming down the last few steps and walking up behind him.

"It's a video I found. I mean it's, um…"

"Sir!" said NutriMom. Her voice suddenly sounded totally alien – toneless, metallic, almost as though it were coming from the speaker atop a storm siren tower. "Did you just call this young boy your 'son'?"

"Holy…!" Emil's father staggered back against the wall, amazed to be addressed directly by the screen. "Emil, what is this?" He pointed. "Who is *she*?"

But now NutriMom's face had disappeared, replaced by a plain black screen with a few words written in bright white.

Emil found that he was able to sound them out for himself with just a little effort.

contacting local security dispatch

Father and son stood face to face inside the shelter, unsure what to say. Emil had meant to tell his dad about NutriMom so many times! Why hadn't he done it? Now, he could see the signs of a new kind of struggle on the older man's face, between anger and something else that was more like amazement.

Perhaps if he tried to explain himself right away, he would have some chance of being properly listened to. Emil gestured toward the screen, and was just about to start talking when his father turned sharply away from him toward the door of the shelter.

"What's *that?*"

Emil didn't notice anything for a second or two. But then he could hear that there was a new sound outside, coming from the direction of the City. It was hardly more than a distant whisper at first, like a light wind rolling in from an advancing Weather front. But after perhaps a minute, while the pair of them stood in silent attentiveness, Emil recognized what it was that he was listening to.

Helicopter blades.

Mark Silcox was born and raised just outside of Toronto, Canada. He has worked as a security guard, a short order cook, and a freelance writer in the video game industry. His writing is featured in the n64 game Aidyn Chronicles: The First Mage and the MMORPG Earth and Beyond. He has doctorate in Philosophy from The Ohio State University, and currently lives in Edmond, Oklahoma, USA

Luxury Underground
Francis Walsh

The last dancehall in America was a bunker.

Built of red brick and rising from among a brace of willow trees, the bunker formed an l-shaped footprint, with the smaller limb above ground and the longer limb buried beneath the earth, and on Friday and Saturday night crowds of locals swarmed through the two metal doors propped open with cinder blocks and descended the quarter-turn staircase to reach the dance floor. The dancers wore whatever outfits they could salvage from their closets or assemble from clothing swaps, and they reveled in their mismatched attire, often lingering in their apartments and laboring in preparation, like Lorraine, who stood in front of her bathroom mirror and posed in a pleather skirt and a Puritan collar blouse sewn in some year before she was born. Ken, wearing wool pants and a microfiber shirt, lurked behind her and tapped a watch on his wrist that no longer ran; he could not fix the mechanism, although he always vowed to. Lorraine knew Ken enjoyed its presence and meaning, and she hurried along to leave the apartment with him.

Outside a poisonous yellow haze filled the air. Ken and Lorraine wore gas masks and walked arm-in-arm, and Lorraine noted how the haze diffused to a dull sepia tone in the torchlights that lined the streets, almost like—

"—an old photograph. Don't you think so? It's very pleasant, it almost makes it seem romantic," Lorraine said, glancing at Ken before quickly looking away—she had never grown accustomed to how the gas mask made Ken look so insectoid, with the bulbous lenses and the drooping canister and the tight rubber hood that rendered him bald, pale, and white. Seeing him made her too self-conscious of her own appearance.

"I don't know," he said, "I always think it looks like the world has been dropped into a puddle."

"Well, that is surely the opposite of what I mean. And you don't have to hold my arm while we walk if you don't want to—no one will think anything of it."

"But I want to maintain appearances. Otherwise, we might end up like that poor fellow, struggling through work just to get new charcoal filters and a crate of peaches," Ken nodded to a conscript-attendant in a white jumpsuit who held an arrow-shaped sign pointing toward the dancehall. All the conscripts wore white jumpsuits. "I hear they only feed the conscripts peaches because they collect the pips to manufacture new filters."

The pair strolled on in silence. An occasional squirrel skittered at the edges of Lorraine's vision while an unseen bird sang a nocturnal song from the branches of a tree that swayed in the evening breeze. No one understood why the animals survived while humans perished, and some people, Lorraine knew, even believed the gas was a ruse.

From behind, Lorraine heard the chime of a bell. Peering over her shoulder, the wall of mist parted and there emerged a pedicab, red with a vinyl canopy and a conscript-attendant positioned in the rear, pedaling furiously, the curved fenders of the bike rattling. As the pedicab rushed past, an arm jutted out of the cab and waved in a smooth arc like a windshield wiper. Rolling to a stop before the dancehall, Dale stepped from the cab; tall and long limbed, Dale wore a wig perched atop his gas mask, and curls of gray hair cascaded down his cheeks. He jostled a hand in his pocket and kicked dirt while waiting for Ken and Lorraine.

"Here comes the private gentleman," Ken said. "The homeowner slumming it."

"Oh, they all 'slum it.' It's to our advantage, really. So be polite. Be your charming self."

"Charming is the only self I bring out on a Saturday night. I keep all my other selves in the closet, you know."

Lorraine knew little of Dale. He was an enthusiastic dancer, if not a technically skilled one. She liked that. Ken enjoyed dancing, but Ken memorized his steps.

Dale, his hands clasped behind his back, stepped forward when Lorraine and Ken approached. To their left was the bunker where the dance had started hours ago and would continue for hours more, and in the air the hum of generators mingled with the muffled thump of the music contained within the bunker. Dale made a slight bow at the waist.

"Good evening. Are you ready for the dance?"

The lenses of Dale's mask reflected the flame of the torchlights, and the brass buttons on his satin breeches and tailcoat glowed. Neither Lorraine nor Ken had ever seen his face.

Dale offered Lorraine his arm and she accepted. The trio approached the door, and the volume of the music increased, the drum beat bounding up the stairs and reverberating off the walls in the above ground entryway. Inside, the music drowned out the whine of the generators, and Lorraine, Dale, and Ken descended the staircase together, where the view of the dance floor bloomed: against the far wall the conscript-deejay in his white jumpsuit had placed speakers that throbbed with music while the overhead track lighting shifted through a spectrum of hot and cool tones—from red to blue and back again—and shone on a cluster of bodies that shook and writhed and kicked and sprayed sweat. Along the wall to Lorraine's right a bartender had set up a fold-out table and overloaded it with canisters of various vapors.

There was no central air system in the bunker—it had been decommissioned as a living space—and Lorraine detached from the two men to take in the view. The turgid air made Lorraine hook a finger in the collar of her shirt before gesturing to the conscript-bartender. The nitrous oxide was free, and Lorraine waited while the bartender affixed a tube to a nipple on her gas mask. She inhaled and floated out of herself for a moment, lifting off with the thrum of a helicopter filling her ears—chuff, chuff, chuff—and afterwards, when she descended, euphoric, she took Dale and Ken by the hand and dragged them toward the crowd, where they slipped in together and moved toward the center. Lorraine closed her eyes and swayed between the two men, picturing herself at the bottom of a well, like a clean drink of water or the shiny coin of a wish maker tossed into the abyss. She thought of wishing upon herself and making her own fortune as she rolled her hips and shoulders to the music.

The music shifted from a rockabilly slap to a hard rock ballad and on to the pop songs of Lorraine's youth ("Hit me baby," she said to Dale, although she was unsure of Dale's age and if the song meant the same thing to him as it did to her) and then the volume of the music lowered and the dancers slowed and the voice of the conscript-deejay rose: he read from a list of the deceased, the conscripts who had perished in accidents that week—a tear in their mask, a clogged generator, an ether overdose, the violence of a private gentleman—as well as the more admirable and serene deaths of old age, those lucky few who had lived out their lives in apartments and had succeeded in raising children and fulfilling their bodily use.

Ken and Lorraine were childless.

While the deejay read the dancers danced, except Lorraine, who slipped away for another whippet. She held a finger up to Dale and Ken and shouldered her way through the crowd. At the bar, Lorraine inhaled, taking flight, both ecstatic and hating the moment, hating the reminder of the relative inconsequence of her life: she would soon be thirty-five and deemed an inefficient procreator. Unless something changed, she would be shuffled off, conscripted, the dances closed off to her except as an attendant.

Her head itched beneath the rubber mask and sweat fogged the lenses. From the sidelines she watched Dale and Ken as they danced back-to-back among the crowd. They would not face each other, although she wondered what that meant in the present circumstances, what with the mask and all. She liked Ken and she pitied Ken. He was a good, if inefficient partner, although she never blamed him. And with Dale, she saw a possibility.

The next morning, Lorraine awoke with her back to Ken. He was curled up like a kidney bean on their twin bed. A circular lamp glowed, synced to brighten with the sun, illuminating the underground room and revealing its contents—Lorraine's skirt, crumpled and circled around the shoes that she had stepped out of the previous evening, and the metal shelving with dry goods, and the sink and the counter, and the round table and chairs, and the clothing chest, and the wall calendar where she had tracked her cycle when they were trying to get pregnant. It came with stickers to ease tracking—red droplets of blood and smiling baby faces. Now the days were blank. A cactus in a stucco pot lived on the table. The room was like one of the many other rooms in a network of underground rooms.

Lorraine rose and stretched. Her head and body ached, and her hair was stiff and matted, so she scooted to the bathroom, unbuttoning the blouse that she had failed to remove before crawling into bed. She turned the knob in the shower stall with the pebbled door and stood beneath the lukewarm water that dribbled from the showerhead. She rested her forehead against the wall and brushed her teeth. She thought of Dale. What did his face look like? Did he have a dimpled chin? Round? Pointed? She spit toothpaste onto her feet, wriggling her toes as the foam swirled away down the drain. She heard Ken moving and she lingered beneath the water.

When she did step out of the shower, she toweled dry and wrapped the towel beneath her armpits before exiting the bathroom. Ken sat at the edge of the bed and sipped instant coffee.

"How was the water today?" Ken asked. It was a question he asked often. A running gag for which she supplied the expected answer:

"Scalding. Unbearable. I nearly cooked."

"We really need to contact the super about that."

Lorraine forced a smile. She left the towel on and wriggled into fresh clothing. Boring clothing. Sweatpants. Everyday wear. She turned her back to Ken and dropped the towel and pulled a sweatshirt over her head.

"You don't have to be so modest," Ken said. "I know things are different now, but it's nothing I haven't seen, and we were—we were—I'm just saying, do whatever makes you comfortable. Don't do it on my account or anything."

"It's not on your account but thank you. How's the coffee today?"

Another running gag that now seemed selfish and myopic in the face of Lorraine's impending birthday—at least they still had the luxury of coffee. She walked over to a calendar to check the date.

"How much time do we have left?" Ken asked.

"Six months. The odds of pregnancy will drop to 29% when I turn 35."

"I'm sure the human body isn't that exacting. I guess it doesn't matter. We can start trying again."

"I don't know. Maybe. I don't want the stress. If these are my final six months before reassignment, I want to enjoy them. It's a life of small comforts, but still a comfort."

Ken stirred his coffee with his finger.

"Where do you think we'll end up later?" Ken said. "Do you really think they stack everyone like sardines in a bunkhouse? I'm not sure I'll be able to sleep."

"I honestly don't know. I've never really spoken to a conscript," Lorraine said, and let the conversation die. Ken showered and Lorraine sat at the table and thumbed through a book, a regency era novel with a heroine who kills herself in the end. So rash and melodramatic. She had read the novel before. Surely there was a different ending somewhere. Ken exited the shower and followed her lead, covering himself as he changed. He reclined on the bed and read a book of his own, whistling absently while he flipped the pages. They listened to the news updates on the radio and the daily announcement reminding them to pledge their bodies, to choose their future, which Lorraine thought sounded like no choice at all.

The light on the circular lamp began to dim and Ken and Lorraine ate instant soup from Styrofoam cups, and Lorraine's nose ran from the steam of the soup, and she went to the bathroom to wash her face, and in the darkening room she wondered again what Dale's face looked like—the curve of his chin, the size of his nose, the fullness of his lips—and when she returned to the living space, Ken lay curled in bed with his back to her, and she crawled in and set her back to his. The room was fully dark now, but she couldn't sleep.

"Ken? Are you awake?"

He stirred.

"What?"

She held her breath and chewed the inside of her cheek.

"I'm going to masturbate."

Ken pulled the blanket up over his shoulders.

"You don't have to ask my permission."

"I'm not asking for permission. I just didn't want to be rude. I figured you would notice and think I was having a nightmare, or a fit, or doing what I was, you know, actually doing and you would feel awkward."

"Do you want to have sex? Try again?"

Lorraine didn't say anything for a moment. Her eyes were open, and she squinted, as if she could find an answer somewhere in the darkness.

"No, I don't think so. It's not that sort of need—did you listen to the news announcement? About pledging one's body. So, I don't know. I was thinking about that."

"A small act of mutiny."

"Maybe. I like you, Ken, but all these years and I've never asked—do you find me attractive?

Ken cleared his throat.

"You're an attractive woman, but I'm not attracted to you."

"That's very diplomatic of you. I suppose it doesn't really matter," she said, and then: "I'll try to be quiet."

Ken shifted closer to the wall, and Lorraine pictured all the possibilities of Dale's chin.

The next day proceeded much like the previous, and the week unfurled before Lorraine in the seemingly endless rhythm of an ocean without horizon. Ken sketched pictures of Lorraine and the cactus, and he seemed content with his fate, but Lorraine felt adrift. At night she did her best to avoid disrupting Ken, and during the day she read books and wandered the underground complex, trailing her finger along the walls and staring dreamily down the hallways, fantasizing about different futures, ones where everything remained unchanged, and ones with children and ones full of loss and white jumpsuits, but they all seemed distant and out of reach. She chatted with her neighbors and exchanged books while waiting in lines at the various depots for powdered milk and canned soup and new charcoal filters, and though an initial burst of excitement accompanied Lorraine's meeting with her neighbors, the dimming prospects of novelty always ferried Lorraine and the other tenants back to their own rooms where the isolation and boredom seemed less pointed without the comparison of someone else's life, which always made Lorraine's heartache—why was she so unhappy with her life of leisure? And if she was unhappy, why was she so scared of a future without this life?

Only one weekly event, the Thursday clothing swap, brought cheer as a reminder of an impending dance, and even then, the exchange itself had become a rote affair, having occurred so often as to render the possibility of a new outfit next to nil; on occasion, however, a new item filtered into the underground bunker, and so Lorraine's heart flowered when she spied a tiara nesting among the clothing. She lifted the headpiece and brought it level to her eyes—it was lightweight and plastic, a simple design of graduated arches studded with rhinestones, costume jewelry, but fanciful, eye-catching, especially to a man in a tailcoat.

This, Lorraine knew, was hers now, and as she set it to her crown, another vision of the future formed in her eye, one that she felt she could guide into existence with a corona of plastic fastened to her head.

Occasionally, Lorraine made the effort of applying makeup before the dance, even though her mask would obscure and smudge the results. At the end of those nights, when she peeled off the rubber that hugged her head, she would invert the mask and see a smeared constellation of her features peering back at her—the blush of her cheeks flanking a set of red lips beneath a black outline of eyes—but when she wore the makeup with the mask she felt as if she could stare through one face and present another, something like—

"—an iceberg." She blotted the inside of her lips with a folded square of toilet paper and then smiled to check her teeth. "Oh, I am sure you know about icebergs, Ken. Like the saying, the tip of the iceberg?"

The bathroom door was open, and Ken sat at the table in the main living space.

"Yes, I am aware of both the natural phenomena and the saying, but I am unsure if others will detect the efforts beneath your mask."

"But I'll know. I will project my face most forcefully. Besides, is it not enough for me to know? Everyone else knowing is mere extra. Frosting, like on—"

"—a cake. Yes. I understand. But how many faces are you peeking through? What's beneath the makeup?"

"That's a bit too arcane for my mind, Ken. Now, will you help me with my tiara?"

Lorraine adjusted the neckline of her shirt and smoothed the chiffon skirt, turning in the mirror and nodding in approval. She stepped from the bathroom and Ken rose and passed her a mask. Like an animal skin, Lorraine thought, slipping the rubber over her face. She knelt before him and he used a small brush to apply glue to the top of her skull, to which he affixed the tiara. He blew, to hasten the drying, and Lorraine stood and thanked him.

"It looks perfect," he said.

They walked, Lorraine taking Ken's arm as they strolled through the halls, ascending a staircase to a door with a conscript-attendant, who spun the wheel lock and gestured for Ken and Lorraine to enter a foyer, shutting the door behind them. The couple stood before another door and waited for a red light to blink green, and they exited the bunker and stepped into the yellow mist. As usual, torches glowered along the roadside.

"Sometimes," Ken said, "I wonder why they bother to do all this—light the torches, enlist the deejay."

"People have always held parties and dances. Besides, it's a—I don't know, an indulgence, I guess. For us. For everyone."

"Not the conscripts."

"I suppose not. But don't go all gloomy on me tonight. I feel like royalty in my little crown and I might have to issue a fiat on unhappiness and doom."

From behind, Lorraine heard the familiar rattle and chime of Dale's pedicab and her heart larruped ahead, quickening even more when Dale's reliable arm protruded from the window and waved. In response, Lorraine lifted her hand and let it hang motionless in the air, a palm-facing hello, and her hand remained in the air as she approached Dale, who complimented her tiara. Her face flushed beneath the mask. He had noticed. The trio linked arms and headed underground. Lorraine guided the men to the vapors table, where she took two inhalations in quick succession before detaching from Ken and hurrying Dale to the dance floor. Ken padded close behind. Lorraine only danced with Dale that night, willing a magnetism to bloom along the points of their hips and joints, and Lorraine wore a smile that she hoped penetrated through the rubber veil of her mask. They danced until the tempo of the music dropped, and then Lorraine and Dale slumped together and heaved for breath. Dale whispered:

"How would you like to take a ride in my pedicab?"

While trundling through the night and cutting through the mist, the pedicab offered little room for two, but Lorraine didn't mind being close to Dale. She sensed that he enjoyed the intimacy.

Dale wrapped his arm around Lorraine and Lorraine nuzzled Dale's shoulder. They rode without speaking and Lorraine felt as if they alone remained motionless, a divine abeyance while the world scrolled past—the trees and the flicker of the torches, the faded lines on the asphalt, the reflected light of a deer's retina, and the few straggling couples dragging each other to the dance. And when the pedicab rolled into the abandoned downtown district, the empty storefronts with boarded windows drifted past, and the unpowered streetlamps marched along. It was as if the whole world consented to move for them. And it wasn't so much romantic to Lorraine as a convergence, the stillness of things settling into place.

She felt the warmth of Dale's body, and her eyes roved over his wig and his mask. His features remained a mystery, a series of possibilities in her mind.

But eventually the pedicab rolled to a stop. They had made a loop and were back at the dance hall. Lorraine had slouched into Dale's body, so she righted herself and blinked beneath her mask when Dale planted a hand on her thigh, right above the knee, and kneaded her flesh. It tickled. The conscript-attendant gulped for breath behind them.

Dale stepped down first. The torchlights leading to the dancehall illuminated his lanky frame, his shoulders slightly slumped, and he offered his hand to Lorraine.

"I suppose you had best return to Ken."

She leaned closer to Dale.

"May I entreat you to keep a secret?"

Dale brushed the hair of his wig back.

"I would not be a gentleman if I could not."

Lorraine chewed the inside of her cheek.

"I would like to see you again. Alone."

Dale stared off toward the dancehall and then turned to face Lorraine.

"It is dangerous, you know. Not that it isn't done, the classes fraternizing. Perhaps I can pick you up sometime during the week?"

People were streaming from the dancehall now. It was getting late, the dance was ending, and behind Dale's shoulder, Lorraine saw Ken shuffling towards them. She looked quickly to Dale and said, well, maybe in a few days then, on Tuesday, and I'll meet you out on this street, just a little way between here and the underground apartments, and right before she turned away to walk home with Ken, Lorraine swore she could see Dale's face staring out from beneath his mask. He was smiling.

Lorraine held the pins in her mouth while Ken stood behind her and bunched the fabric of her dress.

"It's too risky," he said.

"No one will catch me," she mumbled. "We're allowed to go outside. I'm beginning to think you're jealous. Here, help me pin this back."

The dress was blue, with white polka dots, and new to her from the clothing swap, but not the right size. She turned her head and presented the pins to Ken.

"That's not it at all," he said, taking a pin. "I care about you though. What am I doing back here?"

"Fold the fabric over and insert the pin so it goes in and out through both pieces, like a stitch. I guess you don't sew though. Just make sure it holds. I care for you, too. I don't

even know if I like Dale, so much as I like the possibilities he represents."

"What does that mean?" Ken finished with the pins. "How's that look?"

Lorraine ignored the first question and turned in the mirror, craning her neck to inspect Ken's work. Later, after she had left Ken alone in the small square of life that they shared, and after the conscript-attendant driving the pedicab had coasted to a stop and Dale and Lorraine had stepped down to stroll along a lane of elm trees, Dale set a hand on Lorraine's back and a pin lanced his finger. A bead of blood appeared on his skin, and he drew his finger to his mouth before realizing his mistake—his mask was in the way. He laughed and he set his hand lower on Lorraine's back, beneath the pins, and steered Lorraine behind a tree, away from the view of the conscript-attendant. They took a seat on the damp ground at the roots of the tree.

Dale slid his pants down to his ankles, letting the fabric bunch around his boots, not bothering to completely undress. He leaned back and laced his fingers behind his head. His wig was askew and when she slipped the white briefs down along his thighs the elastic waistband left a red ring around his belly. She sat astride Dale and tried to picture his chin, as she had before, and when he drove her home later that evening, Lorraine felt a cooling dampness that cemented not so much as a disappointment but as an inevitably: what choice did she have? She had planned and made a trade that she hoped was in her favor.

Ken was dusting off the cactus with a small paintbrush when she returned home. He didn't look up from his chore.

"This is surprisingly engrossing. I should start a plant spa. How did it go?"

She shrugged.

"It was fine, I guess. You know how those things can be, all the stress and anxiety of anticipation and planning, and then you do it, and—I don't know, then you've done it. It went about how I expected." She slipped out of her shoes and walked over to the calendar, removing it from the wall and flipping backward to the previous months, checking the stickers plastered to different days—the red teardrops, the smiling baby faces.

Ken looked up from the cactus and set his brush aside.

"Is something wrong?"

She tacked the calendar back to the wall.

"No," she said. "I'm going to take a shower."

She stood beneath the dribble of lukewarm water and appreciated the shower for what it was, for what it afforded her—an opportunity to feel something bodily, alone. She could not decide whether this was good or bad, but she knew she had little choice in the matter. Why should she feel ashamed? She had played to expectations. She pictured Dale's chin and then discarded him from a network of possibilities that unfolded in her mind. His chin held no use anymore. She thought of Ken. If she had a child, would he sketch their portrait? She ran a hand along her belly and considered the luxury of her future.

Francis Walsh is a writer from coastal Maine. Their work appears or is forthcoming in Brevity, the Gateway Review, and the Los Angeles Review.

The Call of the Wyld

Twelve grisly tales of fur and fury in this brand new anthology of werewolf stories from Wyldblood press.

- Werewolves on the prowl!
- Werewolves at your door!
- Werewolves in space!
- Werewolves in your nightmares!

All new stories of the night, when the moon is full and the blood drips crimson dark. Tales of loss, hope, adventure and revenge. Wild and weird stories of feasting, stalking, hunting and abandon. Read them in daylight—and lock the doors tight.

Out now £7.99 print £3.99 ebook   www.wyldblood.com/bookstore.

The Bee Tailor
Davin Hall

He stared through the magnifying lens at the delicate structure in front of him. The gash sliced through the outer wing weave and continued through the chitin mesh. He clucked his tongue at the damage and poked around the edges with the point of his tweezers. Several more elements would have to be removed before he could start patching. That meant scraping off adhesive, on top of everything else. For the replacement pieces of wing and exoskeleton, he would need at least two dozen bodies. A costly repair for a pointless exercise, he thought.

"I'm afraid it will be a cost of three hundred and twelve, my lord," the bee tailor said, bowing his head so as not to look above his station.

"Three hundred and twelve?" The young man in front of him made a show of throwing up his hands. "For that tiny mark? That's outrageous."

"I beg your pardon, my lord," the bee tailor said, bowing his head further.

"Three hundred and twelve. Isn't there a warranty?"

"Yes, my lord, but-"

"Well there you are."

"But the warranty does not cover prearranged duels with edged weapons."

"Prearranged?" the young man scoffed. "You think I planned for my dear cousin to have her honor impugned?"

"Of course not, my lord."

"You think I wanted to have a duel at my birthday? Prearranged, he says. Three hundred and twelve. I'll pay two-fifty and nothing more."

"Of course, my lord."

"And have it ready by tomorrow."

"I'm afraid that's quite impossible."

"Do you hear this one?" The young man was probably looking at his companion. "I am leaving the day after tomorrow for hunting. If it isn't ready by that morning, you'll never make so much as a pair of socks again, you hear me? I'll pay three hundred for the rush."

"Of course, my lord."

The young lord and his companion turned and headed out of the shop, talking about the hunting expedition to come. The bee tailor sighed as soon as the door had closed, straightening and wiping a bead of sweat off his forehead. It didn't make him nervous to be around royalty - it was quite common given his line of work - but he disliked the effort it took to have a simple conversation. So many rules to follow, so many protocols to adhere to. It was exhausting. He turned back to the garment on his work table.

It was a beautiful piece, a ceremonial tunic, thousands of bodies in the making. He remembered the moment when he had first dared to lift it up, after he was sure the adhesive had set. Shimmering in the light, he had simply stared at it for several minutes, bending it this way and that to catch the light. The double-layer design was something he was quite proud of, although it did mean the piece should only be decorative. The wing weave was obviously much more fragile than the exoskeleton mesh, but it added such beauty. And the hair extruding through the wings ensured that it was still soft to the touch. Of course, none of that had stopped the young lord from purposing it for a fight.

He sighed again, looking at the slash that cut through all of the hours he had spent bent over his magnifying lens. Despite it all, he had to admit the attack had been a fierce one to break through the chitin. The young lord had been lucky it was a duel and not a fight; his opponent had had a strong arm and a deadly blade. Of course, the bee tailor knew the rumors of who the princess had been consorting with. It had probably all come out at the birthday party, he imagined.

The door to his shop sprang open, and his neighbor, the apothecarist, followed directly after.

"Have a visitor then?" the apothecarist asked, waddling over to his table. The bee tailor raised an eyebrow as his guest. "Come on then," the apothecarist went on. "Was it about the duel? Is that the armor? Good gracious, look at that cut."

The bee tailor frowned. "I can't discuss clients," he said.

The apothecarist hooted in laughter. "Good gracious me, no," he said. "Completely unrelated to any of your clientele, I heard a particular young lord had a duel with another particular young lord of a different house, pertaining to a particular young princess." With each p-word, tiny flecks of spittle ejected from the apothecarist's mouth. He laughed again. "From the looks of it, that particular young lord won't be stepping in the middle of young love again any time soon. I expect we'll be hearing wedding chimes soon enough. Hoo, but he's a scrapper, isn't he? Look at that, right through the armor." He reached for the tunic, and the bee tailor pulled it away. "Need to talk to Queenie then, eh?" the apothecarist asked.

"I expect I will, yes," said the bee tailor.

"Need a refill then?"

The bee tailor clenched his teeth momentarily. "I suppose I will. Not urgently." He busied himself with laying the tunic down and smoothing out the wrinkles.

"Sure, sure," said the apothecarist. "Say, by the end of next week?" The bee tailor looked up sharply, and the apothecarist laughed loudly again. "Don't you fret, I'll get you sorted soon enough. Three days, at most. You can chat away with your lady love to your heart's content." The bee tailor bit his tongue. "I'll let you get to work then, shall I?" said the apothecarist, slowly making his way to the door. "You've got a lot on your table, by the looks of it." He dawdled, waiting to see if the bee tailor would make any other comment. Getting nothing, finally the apothecarist was through the door, and it had closed behind him.

The bee tailor breathed another sigh of relief. While certainly not as burdened by decorum as a conversation with a lord, he found conversations with those at his own station to be tiring as well. There was really only one conversation he enjoyed having.

Making his way to the front door, he locked it and leaned against it for a moment. While it was possible to meet the time constraints placed upon him, the repair would take up all of his time in between now and then. He would be lucky for any sleep he got in the meantime. He made a mental note to remind himself to eat. The worst part was cleaning the wound, so to speak. Removing the damaged pieces of wing and chitin, cutting the silk threads that held the wings in place, and, worst of all, scraping off the adhesive that joined the exoskeletons. It was a tedious process.

But he could make it a little more enjoyable. He went into the back room and put a kettle onto the stove. Retrieving the last package he had received from the apothecarist, he shook it gently. There was enough for three cups, he figured. Possibly four, but he didn't want to push it. Besides, that would be plenty to get him through. He opened it up and scooped a portion of the dry leaves into a cup, inhaling deeply. When he had first received the potion, he had found the smell to be bitter and pungent, like a musty piece of fabric. But over time, he had come to look forward to that smell more and more. He could say he enjoyed the taste of this concoction, when before he had to struggle to gulp it down.

While waiting for the water to boil, he fixed himself a plate with a biscuit with jam to set aside and ensure he had sustenance while he worked. He also carefully put a small dollop of jam off to the side of the plate. It was strawberry, which she said was her favorite, but it was also the only jam she'd ever had. The kettle started to hiss, and he poured the bubbling water into the cup, releasing more of the aroma of the leaves. He breathed in deeply again, before setting the cup down to steep. It needed a few minutes before it was potent.

Taking a sprayer, he exited the shop by the rear door, entering his small courtyard, filled with buzzing insects. He sprayed a few bursts of the gas into the air to relax the bees and made his way to the nearest hive. He doused this with the gas too, and pulled open a small tray. There she was, resting. His queen. Gently, he carried the tray back inside.

He had plenty of bodies for the repair. Honestly, he didn't need to consult with the queen for anything. But it soothed him. With a small spoon, he scooped the queen up and onto the plate, next to the jam. Then, taking both the plate and the tea, he went into his work room.

Sipping the tea, he began to arrange his work station. The solution to weaken the adhesive, the flat knife to work under the chitin pieces, the tweezers to remove the pieces, a small pair of sharp scissors, and the diamond scalpel to scrape away the last bits of adhesive. As the potion began to take effect, he heard a faint buzzing around the room, from any creature, no matter how small, that happened to be nearby. A small group of ants were making inroads on his windowsill, and he politely asked them to remain outside. Eventually though, the potion's effects tightened to their intended goal, his ability to converse with a specific individual. She was still sleepy from the gas, but was rousing.

"Hello, my dear," the bee tailor said, as he began working on the tunic. "I've some jam for you, when you're feeling up for it. It's just next to you." He edged the flat knife under a chitin piece and began to slowly pry it up.

"Hm?" The voice was soft, like the hair that covered the tunic. It emanated inside his head, silky and gentle, like warm flowing water. When he had drunk the potion for the very first time, he thought the voice would come from the source, as one might expect. He hadn't known that the magic simply placed the queen's thoughts into his own head. It had taken a moment to get used to, but now he thought of her voice inside his mind like a gentle caress.

"I can understand her, that's very well," he had said to the apothecarist. "But how can she understand me?"

"It translates," was all he had said.

He still didn't fully understand, but the effects certainly worked.

"Jam?" she whispered, still groggy.

"Mmhmm. Next to you," he repeated.

"Thank you." He glanced over and saw her crawl to the jam, dipping her head to it. In the next moment, his mind filled with the joy she felt at the sugary treat, and he beamed.

"How are you feeling?" he asked, focusing back on the tunic. He pried a piece of broken exoskeleton off.

"I'm well, thank you," she said. He felt her settling on the plate, relaxing. "How are you? Busy?"

"Mm," he nodded. "Very. Someone has managed to get stabbed while wearing one of my pieces."

"Oh my goodness," she said, with alarm. "Was the person hurt?"

"No, no. Just a duel."

"I don't understand."

"A duel? Um, when they fight, the blades are hexed so that-"

"Hexed?"

"A spell is placed on them. Magic."

"Ah."

"And so the blades can't cut flesh. Well, not deeply. They mark the victim, to indicate a point was won."

"I see."

He continued on to the next piece.

"Why do they fight, if they do not intend to hurt each other?"

"Well," the bee tailor said. He enjoyed talking like this, his mind split between the two tasks, the work at hand and the conversation. He found he didn't have to over-think what he wanted to say, he could simply speak freely. "They fight for honor, I suppose. I think there was a question about a young woman in this case. A princess."

"I see," the queen said. She was quiet for a moment. "Could they not perform some other competition for their honor?" she asked. "One in which their tunics were not harmed? Or that did not involve blades?"

"I suppose they could," said the bee tailor. "But they do enjoy their customs, don't they?" He chuckled softly.

"It makes me very sad when any of my bees fight each other," said the queen. The bee tailor nodded, absentmindedly. "They fight to the death," she said. "Could you not play a game? A game of chess?"

He chuckled again. He had tried to teach her chess several months ago, and while she had grasped the concept, not being able to fully see the board presented too much of a problem. "Yes, they certainly could," he said. "But they like the combat. They like the idea of death, especially when there is no threat of it. And so they choose their test of skill accordingly."

"But it leaves you with much work, does it not?"

"Mm," the bee tailor nodded. "It can. It has in this case, anyway."

"And it is not necessary."

"I suppose not."

"A waste of your time."

He nodded again. "I do get paid though," he said. She was silent. He knew she didn't quite understand money and its function.

"A waste," she paused. "Of their money?"

"That it is," he said, leaning back and stretching his neck. "But they have plenty to waste. It means very little to them."

He could feel her working through the confusion. "What has little meaning to them, has great meaning to you?"

"Yes," he said. "That's a good way of putting it."

"Does this upset you?"

He looked over at her. "Why would you ask that?"

"It is an imbalance," she said.

The bee tailor stared at the insect laying on the plate. "I suppose it is. Um, yes, it does upset me, now that you bring it up. It upsets me to see people treat something so casually that other people, including me, hold dear." He sensed her affirmation, as if she had nodded.

He set the damaged pieces of exoskeleton aside. They could be boiled down to turn into glue later on. For now, the broken pieces of wing needed to be removed, but this was an easier process. While the queen returned for a second helping of jam, he deftly cut the silk threads holding the wings in place, and tied off the ends so the strands wouldn't unravel.

He brushed the wing fragments into a small pocket of the table for refuse. Now came the unfortunate process of scraping, and he grudgingly picked up the diamond scalpel and set to it.

The next morning, he brought the queen into the workshop again, and settled her in place with jam while he drank his tea.

"Good morning," he said.

"Good morning."

"Sleep well?" the bee tailor asked.

"Yes, thank you."

He carefully set the tray of gassed bees to the side. He had more than he needed, so he could be a little choosy. The larger ones would help the process go a little faster, and the smaller ones were useful for filling in odd spaces. Looking back and forth between the torn garment and the bodies, he selected a bee and picked it up with his tweezers. Placing it in the special cradle, he used the tweezers to pinch the head off, followed by the wings. The wings he set aside. Next, taking his tungsten scalpel, he severed the abdomen, and began to cut along the side of it, separating the hard upper exoskeleton from the rest of the body.

"How is the work progressing?" asked the queen, suddenly.

"Hm? Oh, it's early yet, so hard to say. But I think it's starting off well. This fellow is cooperating."

"What was the fight about?"

"I'm sorry?"

"The fight. That led to the damage. Do you know the particulars?"

The bee tailor blinked, distracted. It was unlike the queen to ask questions like this. She seemed to be in a strange mood today. "Well," he said, gathering his focus again and turning back to peeling away the exoskeleton. "Let's see. The daughter of the emperor, that would be the ruler of this land, is betrothed to someone of a, let us say, a different nature. Someone from a barbarian clan." He thought about the best way to help her understand this. "The barbarians, they are to us, to someone like me, as a wasp might be to you. Do you know wasps?"

"Of course."

"Bigger, stronger, more ferocious. Quite ugly, I would add, although the princess appears not to share my view." He chuckled to himself. The queen did not recognize the source of humor. "Anyway," the bee tailor continued. "The young lord who was wearing my tunic insulted this barbarian, who did not take kindly to the offense."

"What was the reason for the insult?" interrupted the queen.

"No reason," said the bee tailor. "Simply that he was a barbarian."

"But that is his nature, is it not? He cannot be anything but a barbarian, so to insult him for this is foolish."

The bee tailor chuckled again. "I suppose it is," he said. He had finished peeling the exoskeleton off the first bee and set it aside, starting to work on the second one. He couldn't be sure of how many he would need in the end, but he would start with two dozen and hope that they covered it. "But there it is. We insult others for how they are. Do bees not share a similar behavior?"

"We do not," the queen said, a bit insulted herself to be even asked the question, it seemed to the bee tailor.

"A noble quality," said the bee tailor. "If we humans shared more of it, I would not have to be straining my eyes on repairing this tunic."

"I do not find wasps to be ugly," the queen said.

The bee tailor shook his head. She certainly was in a strange mood today. "No?" he said, smiling to himself. "Attractive to you, are they?"

"I do not find them beautiful nor ugly. I find them to be as they are."

"What do you find beautiful then?" asked the bee tailor.

The queen was silent for a moment. "Blooming flowers," she said, finally. "Flowers and the sun."

"Hm," the bee tailor grunted approvingly, slowly peeling back the second exoskeleton. "Those are quite beautiful," he said. Sometimes he wondered if the work would go faster if he segmented the steps even further. First slicing off the heads of each bee, then the wings, then incising around the exoskeleton, and so on. Perhaps he could train an apprentice in some of these tasks. Certainly in decapitating the bees, that would hardly take much skill.

The work continued in silence for some time. There was a strange feeling coming from the queen, like a sort of introspection. The bee tailor was hesitant to disturb her. But there was also a feeling of sadness coming from her.

"You know," he said. "I find you quite beautiful."

This seemed to snap her out of her thoughts. "You do?" she said.

"Oh, yes," he said. "Very much so. And I enjoy our talks a great deal. You're a lovely conversationalist." He smiled.

"Thank you," she said. And the feeling of sadness returned, stronger than before.

It was very late. He estimated only a few hours before the sky started to lighten with the dawn. There was no telling when the lord would be by in the morning to pick up his mended garment, but the bee tailor knew he could be done in an hour's time. He might even be able to get a few winks of sleep. He had finished placing the exoskeletons, and had brushed everything with an extra layer of adhesive. The chitin resin would take a day or so to fully harden, but as long as the young lord didn't go insulting anyone while traveling to go hunting, there should be no problem. A few wings needed to be stitched in, and then he would finally be done. He restrung a needle with silk, and took another drink of tea.

"How is the repair going?" asked the queen.

"Very well," the bee tailor said. "Almost finished." He squinted through the magnifying lens, carefully placing the next wing in place.

"And then?"

"What's that?" the bee tailor asked, distracted.

"What then?" asked the queen.

"He should be by in a few hours to pick it up."

"I apologize," the queen said. "I meant, what will your next project be?"

"Next project?" He was getting punchy from sleep deprivation, he could feel it. It was harder to keep his work and a conversation going at the same time. "A pair of gloves," he said. "Dueling gloves, as it so happens."

"Another duel?"

"Well, the customer doesn't have one planned, as far as I know. But I'm sure one will turn up in good time."

"A duel for honor?"

"Presumably," the bee tailor said. "They usually are."

"A duel where no one is hurt."

It wasn't a question, but he hadn't noticed. "Usually not, no. Accidents can happen."

"How many-" she stopped in the middle.

"What's that?" he asked, looking up.

"How many of my children will you require?"

He blinked in surprise, stopping what he was doing, holding the threaded needle in one hand and tweezers in the other, he stared at the queen. She had never asked that question before. "How many-" he dumbly repeated.

"How many of my children will you require?" she asked again.

"Oh, well," he paused. They had discussed his work before. She knew what he did and how he did it. But she had never asked such a direct question about it in regards to the bees he used to make the products. "I would say around two hundred," he said, hesitantly.

"Two hundred," she said, calmly.

"Yes?" He was entirely unsure of himself. The way the question had been asked had thrown him. She had been so matter-of-fact, but underneath the question had been something else. There was just a glimpse of it, a negative feeling. The effects of the potion allowed him to converse with the queen, and since it was a telepathic connection, it also conveyed a general sense of emotions that she was experiencing, but the process wasn't perfect. The spell was designed for language, not feelings, and the emotions were faint or muddled or both. But something had been there. Something like fury.

"Why?" she asked.

"We've been over this," the bee tailor said. He was starting to feel annoyed now. He didn't have anything to feel guilty about, this was his profession. He was an artist. The queen knew all of this already, why was she making a fuss now? "I use the wings and the exoskeleton of the bees to make clothing, armor."

"But why?" asked the queen again. "Are there no other materials you could use?"

"These are highly prized garments," the bee tailor said, more snappish than he had intended.

"But are there no other materials?"

"Of course there are other materials! But these are rare! The material is strong but comfortable and beautiful to look at. My work is worn at the highest ceremonial functions in the land. And it has been sent to kings in distant lands as well. No one else has the skill to work with these materials! I am an artist." He dropped the needle and the tweezers and glared at the queen. It was about time to send her back to her shelf.

"There is no reason for their destruction," the queen said.

He picked up the plate, less gently than he usually did. "Time to go back," he announced.

"There is no reason for the duels," she said.

The bee tailor carried her through the work room, through the living quarters.

"Their bodies have such little meaning to you," she said.

"Now hold on," the bee tailor said, stopping at the door that led outside. "They have a great deal of meaning to me. Without them, I don't have a livelihood. I am a respected and revered artist. Without your children, without you, I have none of that, and I'm just a nobody."

"A nobody?"

"Yes!"

"Without their bodies, you would have no body?"

"What in blazes are you talking about?" The bee tailor was furious, and the thoughts coming from the queen were coming all in a jumble. The emotions were ranging all over, or maybe they were becoming mixed with his own. He couldn't decipher the blend. Here was the fury, and there a deep sadness, and then pity. He opened the door and stormed into the courtyard, not bothering to use the gas to calm the bees. It was late and they would be mostly asleep, apart from a few guards. It was no matter if they stung him, he'd been stung before. Let them martyr themselves on him.

"Their bodies have meaning to you," the queen said as he approached the hive. "But their lives do not. Do you understand?"

He pulled the shelf open where her throne room was. "I understand you do not appreciate my work," he said. "And I understand what perhaps you do not, that it doesn't matter what you think."

"I understand," said the queen. "I understand there is nothing I can do but beg."

"What?" The bee tailor was about to tip the queen onto the shelf, but stopped.

"Please," said the queen. Her soft voice was calm. "Please do not hurt my children. I cannot stop you. I cannot force you. I would, if I could. I would do everything it takes to save them. Please. Please help me."

The bee tailor stared at the small insect. Small bits of biscuit and jam were still on the plate. She looked ridiculous, now that he thought about it. Laying there, helpless like that, surrounded by bits of food. A queen? Queen of what? What did she have? Who was she to make such a request? Who was she to chide him? His jaw tightened and his eyebrow twitched.

"Please," she said again, and he felt an overwhelming sadness rush over him. Her feelings were of despair, hopelessness, powerlessness, and a crushing dread. His jaw unclenched.

"I, I cannot," he whispered. "It is impossible."

"I see," said the queen. She lay very still. "I will not speak to you again," she said.

The bee tailor watched, as if someone was controlling his arm, as he slowly deposited the queen back onto the shelf and slid it back into the hive. A few bees were flying around him, but they returned to their posts. He stared at the hive, still receiving the emotions of the queen. She was grief-stricken, for her fate, for her children's fate, and something else. He sensed it. She felt such sadness for

him, for his failure, for his complicity. Even as he stood there, he felt the grief start to subside. It didn't completely dissipate, and now he felt joy. The joy at being home and surrounded by her children. She understood everything, understood the cause for which they were being sacrificed was an utterly pointless one, understood that she was powerless to prevent it. Understood his failure to choose the right path. She understood these things and still found joy.

The bee tailor turned and went back to his work room to finish the garment. The young lord would be arriving soon.

Davin Hall is a former law enforcement analyst who saw the light and is now trying to see if this whole "follow your dreams" thing is a good idea. He lives in Greensboro, North Carolina, USA and writes about policing at davinhall.medium.com. Follow him (or not) on Twitter at @geogeng.

Thought Surgery
Richard Webb

I never liked my nose. Hate it, actually. It's big and wonky. My looks are cursed all round in fact. I have thinning hair, I'm on the short side, (dumpy too), but I particularly hate my nose. I stare at it in the mirror as if staring down a nemesis. The hours I spend imagining it was different, wishing I could change it…

… and then gradually, so, so slowly… I do.

I don't believe it at first. I'm in a hurry, getting ready for another evening of abject social failure. I glance at my reflection. Barely noticeable, but my nose *is* just a little straighter. I stop, check the mirror. Perhaps a little smaller too. No—I'm just being hopeful, fooling myself. I leave the house, annoyed. Whatever else I may be, I'm not delusional.

As the night wears on I put it out of my mind, refuse to look at myself in the mirror in the pub. Makes little difference—no-one else looks at me either. I put on a brave face on, (my usual mask). I get drunk, pretend I'm having fun. My friends are loud, lewd and full of laughter. I wonder if any of them have the same worries behind their leering grins. I go home, alone, crash asleep on my bed, knowing my head and my heart will hurt in the morning.

I awake with a start. My head explodes. I wilt back onto the pillow until the pain subsides to a nagging but manageable throb. I find a glass of water by my bedside and take a few gulps. My mouth is dry and sour, my guts are churning and I'm pretty sure I smell rank. Why do our bodies betray us so badly?

I feel sick. I stagger upright, then forward and sideways at the same time towards the bathroom, heaving up a torrent of bitter bile into the toilet. I wipe the bowl, shaking, wretched. Eventually I drag myself upright. My eyes find the mirror. Never have I seen such an appalling, pathetic face looking back at me, begging for pity. Stupid, stupid face. I want to tear it off.

But my nose *is* a little smaller!

I try to shake myself out of my turgid torpor and look at it again. It is definitely smaller; straighter too—pretty normal-looking really. I haven't imagined it. Yes, well, actually I have *imagined* it. Or wished for it, many times, over many years. Either way it is undeniable. After all, is there any harsher truth-teller than a mirror?

Have I been punched, is it broken? It doesn't appear so, nor is it painful, though the thud in my head might be blanking out all other sensations. If I am honest, I'm quite likely to get punched in the face—people have been close to doing so before. Booze never makes me the life and soul exactly; life and *asshole* perhaps. But anyway, my nose is not broken; in fact it is… perfect!

I grin. My teeth show crooked in the mirror. I stop smiling and stare at my reflection. At my mouth. Why are my lips so thin, my teeth misaligned? I imagine something more pleasing: fuller, symmetrical, with a hint of playfulness, with gleaming white teeth standing straight and neat, perfectly sized and placed. I wish I could change them…

I stare at my mouth in the mirror, all the while keeping that perfect picture in my mind. I go into a kind of trance, blocking out everything else. I rarely think this hard about anything. Eventually the buzz of the migraine inside my head swells to a roar so I have to stop, but I swear I feel a tingle in my lips.

Later that day, once my hangover erodes, I try again. I feel the sensation in my lips once more, so I keep going.

After a few days I think I can see change happening. As much to convince myself of my madness as anything, I search through old photos to compare against. There are not many and even fewer in which I actually smile—mostly I stare in resentment at the photographer—but eventually I find one. In it, I am laughing, caught unawares. I barely recognise myself.

I stare at it, holding it up to the mirror alongside the reflection of my face. I look from one to the other, back and forth. My eyes compare my mouth and nose in the photo to that in the mirror, reducing them to abstract shapes. I scarcely believe it at first—who doesn't want to believe their face is more pleasing than it really is? But it is *true*, objectively so: the pictures are different, my face *is* now different. Somehow, I have wished it into being. The change is subtle, yet marked to me, knowing each contour of my own despised face as well as I do.

I wonder at the nature of this change: is it faith, or magic, or science? I have cast no spells, nor spoken any prayers. Have I opened some dormant part of my mind, or did a god help me to do so? Have I unknowingly become a mage (or even a deity)? I don't feel magical or godly. I'm too rational to believe any of this but isn't this how people of faith believe everything was created: by matter being 'thought into existence' by the gods? And now, I can do it too—well, a little bit at least.

Evidence is required. I grab my phone and take a picture, brushing aside the weird realisation I have just taken my first 'selfie.' I create a file, upload the photo and set a password. This is for my eyes only. I call the file 'ChrysalisOne.'

Travelling to work, I receive further proof. The sun is shining and everyone around me is shining too, in the twinkle of their eyes, the gloss of their hair or the sparkle of their teeth. Everyone looks good, glowing with inner confidence. I shuffle onto the bus, embarrassed to be amongst them—an intruder. I stand, holding the rail, squeezed too close to other bodies and lurching with the whims of the damned vehicle. (Buses are so bloody degrading).

A woman nearby—young and full of shine— looks at me. *Properly* looks at me, catching my eye. She doesn't look away, at least not immediately. A wry smile crinkles the corner of her mouth and she arches one of her eyebrows, just a hint. I know I haven't imagined it. This is unprecedented! I think of little else all day and rush home that evening, to get back to the mirror, to my task. 'Project ChrysalisOne' has been green-lit.

I practice, finding ways of improving my concentration, locking onto images of desired changes in my head. I stare without blinking at my reflection, projecting the next modification. It is just like exercise: the benefit is imperceptible at first, painful too, but progress comes. The following day my mind aches with the effort of it but I know I must work through this. Man up, man: no pain, no gain.

Over time, I get better, faster at effecting alteration, like building up a muscle or speeding up reflexes. Turns out you can improve how hard you think if you think hard enough about it!

I face-off against my own face. The sense of contest is important: I wrestle against myself. My reflection is my arena but also my prize. The mirror becomes my friend or team-mate when it is working, my opponent when it is not. Ibuprofen becomes my regular post-workout masseur. I can manage several sessions each day if I manage the pain right.

I plan it all out. I draft a program of self-improvement; one thing at a time. Face first: nose—done; mouth—in progress; then jawline, then cheekbones, eyes, and skin. Maybe ears too, though mine are actually okay. (No-one really looks at ears, do they?)

The work is hard. Sometimes my mind fuzzes over, unable to hold the right image for long enough. I sit on the edge of the bath, searching images of famous, good-looking men, seeking the right reference material: this is essential research, (and not *at all* weird). I scan for shots of film stars, sports stars, pop stars... men who are rich, successful, *desired...* it's all in their looks. Isn't it?

It all takes months, but gradually I work my strange mind-magic. My face is reshaped, millimetre by millimetre. I am like a 'claymation' film animator studiously manipulating the pose of a clay model the merest fraction between each painstaking shot. After each day I upload a new selfie to ChrysalisOne. From one day to the next, there is no difference. But comparing back to a picture from, say, three weeks ago, the difference is noticeable—to my eye at least.

Over time, I overcome my complexion, fighting the details of every tiny blemish. I conquer one patch of skin, sometimes within minutes, only for a new battle to break out somewhere else the next day. But I win in the end.

"What is your regime?" a woman at work asks me.

I frown, acting innocent. "Regime?"

"Yes, your skin; looks great," she says. She shares a little awkward smile and runs a finger through her hair. "Is it a special skin crème you use?" I laugh this off. My 'regime' is simple: no more skin care, no more diets, no more wrinkles... it's all in the mind, though of course I don't say so.

Over a few more weeks I sort my hair out, for once and for all. The tangled mousy mop is gradually swapped out for thick black locks, with a healthy-looking gleam. The hair I always wanted; the hair I *deserve.*

Because I'm worth it.

I get a haircut. The cut is not perfect, (despite me presenting the barber with a photo of George Clooney to copy), but after a week of intense focus, I make it so. With a little concentration each day, I can ensure it never loses style, never gets longer, and never needs another cut. No combing, no gel or products, just a little bit of 'me time' to keep it right. A good hair day, every day, forever.

Perfection, once achievable, is intoxicating. I decide to remove the stubble from my chin. It takes about a week of careful concentration, up close to the mirror with magnifying glass in hand, killing off one hair at a time. Once that is done, I never need to shave again either. I'm saving a fortune on razorblades!

"Like your hair," says the woman at work. She talks to me most days now. We have worked in the same office, two desks apart, for three years, with barely a word between us. A month ago she introduced herself to me as Sophie. "And the new colour really suits you." In a few weeks she'll have forgotten my hair was ever any other colour.

"Do you think I should change *my* hair colour?" She looks sheepish as she asks, again running her fingers through her locks as she looks at me.

"I like it as it is," I reply. She tries not to smile too much and blushes a little, I notice.

After several months I look far better than ever before. I overhear people at work wondering in whispers whether I've 'had work done.' Some might think of it as cosmetic surgery but what I do is so much more than that. It is 'thought surgery,' and it is me waking up to my inner voice, not paying for someone with a scalpel to fashion a dream from my flesh. I have found the means of peeling back my outer husk. I will emerge from my cocoon reborn, shining and new, magically remade.

One night I spring awake, shaken by a nightmare. In it, I am a were-creature, a shape-shifter, transforming in slow-motion into something hideous and malcontent. The images unnerve me. Am I a monster of someone's creation, now unbound?

I am jittery and try to put the nightmare from my mind by reaching for my phone beside the bed. I open ChrysalisOne and run the file of photos through an app which puts them into a slideshow. The pictures document my change, from loathed to loved.

I shudder at the early shots, no longer recognising the person with the pleading eyes trying to avoid the lens. I prefer the later ones, looking coolly to camera—much more palatable. Watching the slideshow is like watching a horror movie with a happy ending and I sleep much better after that.

Nights out improve immeasurably. Women now look at me. All the time. I even take one home now and again. (And yes, if you must know, I did give myself an extra inch or two in a certain area—a Christmas present to myself. Well, you would, wouldn't you? Be *honest* now).

I rarely drink these days. Don't feel the need to. One night at a bar, I am chatting to a couple of women when I notice this guy, alone, gulping down a whiskey, staring at me. He's pissed off. I recognise that look. It's the one I used to wear. I ignore him; it's what he deserves. He leaves, huffing.

He is waiting for me outside. "Oi, pretty boy," he says. "Think yer bloody it, don't ya?" He is drunk, slurring and stumbling. "Think yer so special." He belches and I think for a second he might vomit.

"Whatever," is all I say in reply.

"Smug bastard. Betcha couldn't fight a proper man like—" He staggers towards me, swinging his arm. He misses and snarls.

I know why he wants to punch me. He's the old 'me.' Pathetic. It is himself he really wants to punch. He gives me a shove. I shove back, harder. He's so drunk, he topples. I walk off, unhurried, not looking back as he sobs on the pavement.

I think about it later, admitting that it could have been more serious, and wondering if perhaps I should get myself a bit more conditioned. Yes, I'm pretty well-honed these days, (thanks to staring at a photo of Hugh Jackman's abs all summer whilst staring at my own), but that is of little use in a fight.

Should I try to make my jaw rock-hard or my fists as strong as iron? I wonder to myself how far I could take it with these, *less natural* self-improvements. This is just comic-book super-hero stuff though, isn't it? But what if I *could* make myself more of a man than other men? What if I could achieve a new level of augmentation—shouldn't I be looking beyond notions of just *good-looking*? Maybe I should be thinking bigger, something more high-performance—a 'super-powered' body, maybe? Faster, stronger—bigger perhaps. Indestructible! Or something else, something different? How far could my magic go? For now, I just hold these thoughts in the back of my super-powered mind.

In the meantime, I enhance my bodywork, broaden my shoulders and put a little more beef on my biceps. Of course, I have to be bare-chested when I'm staring at the mirror. It used to feel a little ridiculous, but I know it works. I've learned to appreciate the company of the guy looking back at me. He nods his approval as we flex our arms in perfect synchronicity. What a guy! He's no longer my nemesis. In fact, I love him more than ever.

I think I'd like to be a little taller as well. After all, I'm dark and handsome now, may as well get the full set. Major improvements such as these take longer though, as I have to visualise the bone and muscle under the skin in order to lengthen my back and limbs. (I even have to resort to looking at medical diagrams to help my mind focus). The toll is agony, but I bear it in private and the tramadol helps for a while, though I might need to think about something stronger in the long run.

While I'm looking at myself looking at the mirror, I get a little lost sometimes. Which one am I? Have I have stepped out of the mirror or has another man stepped out of me? The guy in the mirror, (I think it is him), looks at me and smiles, shaking his head, letting me know I need to snap out of it.

Sophie invites me to sit with her in the work canteen sometimes, but not always—

she's careful not to appear too keen in front of gossiping colleagues. She leans towards me and asks: "Have you been working out?"

"Yes," I reply. In my head, not in a gym, but I don't tell her that.

"Good for you." She is quiet for a while, sipping a soda. "Maybe we could… I dunno, maybe you'd like to work out with me, y'know, sometime, if you're not busy."

"That would be… nice," I say.

Nice. I rush home from work to spend more time looking at myself in the mirror, trying to wish all my planned-for changes into being all at once. It's a hard-core workout, and I am *pumped.* Sometimes I think so hard I break sweat.

I've worked at the same place for five years now and I have a meeting the HR manager. I think she wants to promote me—my colleagues say such positive things about me these days.

"It says here in the file, that you're thirty-seven. But that can't be right," she says.

"I *am* thirty-seven." It hadn't occurred to me to lie about this.

Her expression betrayed her amazement. "I expected you to be… " Her voice trails off, before she betrays her professionalism.

Younger.

And no, I don't look my age. After all, I have removed all my wrinkles and blemishes. My body has no trace of middle-aged spread or sagging skin. My once-thinning hair is now thick lustrous, without a hint of grey. I am rejuvenated, remade, reborn.

"What age did you think I was?" I ask.

She is embarrassed, glossing over the matter by changing subject and talking shop.

I'm not paying attention, lost in my thoughts. Until now, I hadn't considered it but to all intents, *I have* got younger, as those around me get older—I am no longer ageing. Has my mind mastered time as it has mastered my body? I'm cheating time, at least on the outside, and in this world it's what is on the outside that counts. It decides what the world decides about me. Your face is your reality check. Mine has become my painting in the attic.

Call it wishful thinking. A thought experiment. Mind over matter. Will to Power. Somehow, I have accessed a higher form of thinking. Perhaps *I* am a higher form. In fact, I am sure of it. I have unlocked my inner Übermensch.

One day at home I find a photo of my former self in a drawer I'm clearing out. I'm on the short side, dumpy, with thinning hair and a crooked smile that doesn't reach my eyes. I stare out of the picture, desperate for the picture-taker to point the camera elsewhere. And, my god, that *nose*. I feel sick. It is not embarrassing, so much as depressing. I can't look at it. I can't let anyone else look at it either. I rip it up. The few photos of myself on the walls of my flat came down a long time ago but I feel an overwhelming urge to find all the others. I rummage through drawers, cupboards, wardrobes, finding old albums and loose photos. I end up ransacking my flat, hunting down the old me.

I have them all. Putting the photos in the kitchen sink and setting them ablaze, I think I should be sad but these pictures show a different person. His eyes tell of despair and loneliness. He tried hard in his way, I suppose, craving acceptance—so eager to please others. No self-belief though, always thinking the worst of himself rather than thinking the best and making it so. The flames purge me of his taint but my head throbs until I gulp two codeine tablets. There is more work to be done: I go online. Deleting all trace of him will make my awakening complete. All surgery requires a period of recovery; this is my after-care, my recuperation therapy.

Click, delete; click, delete; click, delete.

After the obvious imperfections have been taken care of, I start on all the tiny things that didn't bother me previously, just because I can: the curve of my fingernails; the size of my ankles; and yes, the shape of my ears.

I work on the colour of my eyes. I mean, they're okay, but I'm sure I could do better. I go from muddy brown to a mesmeric light green in instalments, working my way through a palette of shades in between. No-one notices the work-in-progress; after all, how familiar are you with the eye-colour of anyone else? (Test yourself, you won't remember many, I promise). I keep going until I get the colour I want.

"I never noticed you had such green eyes before," says Sophie, one day at work. I smile, flashing the pearly whites which go with them. She smiles back, lost in my eyes, hypnotised. Nowadays when I turn it on I get the same response pretty much all round, regardless of age, gender, preferences: I charm them all. I have off-the-chart charisma and I don't even have to try.

It's too easy.

I don't need to be witty or smart or good at my job or even particularly pleasant—everyone is willing to give me a break. I experiment with lateness, sloppiness in my work, rudeness even, smiling all the while, a twinkle in my eyes. It's fun at first, seeing how far I can push it. No-one has a comeback; perfection wins every time.

I float through my day on a cloud of other people's reactions: admiration, eagerness, envy, desire—all provide the fuel to keep me energised. Even outright hatred, (which is really just powerless jealousy), keeps me powered up. But never indifference—that's the only thing I can't bear.

Notice me.

People will never see me the same way. After a while I don't see them the same way anymore either. I mean, all their imperfections—why don't they do something about them? Do they never think to try? Really *think*, that is.

They start to bore me. Their reactions become predictable—always positive, always wanting my attention in return for theirs.

How long can anyone remain interested in a game they can't lose?

I barely go to the office after a few more months. Even Sophie has lost her shine to me. Despite my utter dereliction of duty somehow the HR manager never quite manages to give me my notice so I'm still on the payroll for now. It means I can spend more time at home. I've had mirrors installed in every room, so I can get some work in wherever I am: lying in the bath, standing in the kitchen. As long as I have enough tramadol to keep the headaches at bay I can go for hours at a time. I never get bored of looking at myself.

As time passes, I change more and more; sometimes I could swear I can see things change in front of my eyes. Revolution, not just evolution.

But the thing about an unlimited palette is that you don't know where to stop. There is no stop. Perfect face: sure; perfect body too. But that is the thing with perfection: it leaves you very dissatisfied after a while.

I am beyond other people by now. Their opinions, flattery, rewards and relationships mean little to me. I have moved beyond being just a man. There is no ceiling. I look to the skies. I will become more than human.

I take myself to the brink, to the edge of the world. I stand, toes curled over the edge of the tower, feeling the wide open space of the plains below. The panorama is breath-taking. As I survey all before me, I notice a small boy in a blue coat in the park way, way below. He stands, holding his bike, looking directly up at me. He waves.

I feel the wind through my wings, gusts fluttering their feathers. They took months, far longer than any of my 'human' augmentations. They cost me much—I endured many nights of anguish as they sprouted from my shoulders, feeling like their weight would tear my spine apart. I got no sleep for a month, just lying on my bed, trying not to scream as I stared at the mirrors on my ceiling, willing the change into reality. Even the morphine I procured from a nurse in return for a date gave me only minor respite from the pain. Yet I proved to myself I was strong enough. I kept my focus, plastering downloaded images of the eagle's skeleton and musculature on my walls, so I could study and recreate each limb and articulation.

Then the adjustments: realigning my shoulders and broadening my rib-cage and upper torso to compensate for the extra load. I ground my teeth through the torment as I ground out the results I wanted. Then came muscle, then feathers; hundreds, thousands of them—each sharp tine taking ten minutes of focused imagining to break through my skin but my concentration never wavered, even though my eyes streamed. I could no longer leave the house, so I ordered my meds online, stockpiling them until the pharma company refused to deliver any more.

Re-learning to walk, spread and re-fold my wings, even learning to sleep with them— all those processes took time. But it has all been worth it for this moment: the moment I prove humans can evolve, upwards, become greater. The moment I become more than myself.

I take a selfie and upload it to my ChrysalisOne file.

I flex the muscles from my upper back through my shoulders and along my new limbs. My wings fully extend. I can already feel the wind pulling at them, tantalising, urgently demanding the release from gravity but I lean back, holding it in, savouring the sensation. I breathe deeply, feeling the confidence and satisfaction flow through me, fresh and delectable. I stand on the summit, in more ways than one. I am overwhelmingly proud of myself. Like a high-diver, I raise myself up on my toes, bend at the knees and push off…

I soar. I surf across the crashing waves of air, riding the thermals and shooting the breeze. The wind rushes torrents under my wings. I glide on exhilaration, free as a bird.

No-one has over done what I am doing right now. No-one. This is mine, not for those lower people. The sun beams on my face and I close my eyes.

Something is wrong. The wind is dropping. I have no control. I can move my wings but realise I don't really know how to use them. I flick them out but they are not at the correct angles to propel me. How did I get them wrong? I am losing height. I try again but it is still all wrong, slowing me down rather than generating momentum. I panic, flapping wildly, without rhythm or purpose.

Down, down…

I see treetops as I plummet, first a blur of green, then individual trees. My limbs move but everything is out of synchronicity. I can't breathe, can't focus. Nothing works, nothing can help me. I am sucked from the sky, gravity's plaything.

Down, down…

I crash into the first tree, pure white pain exploding through me. A rush of branches snap, bones break, and my breath is punched from me. I fall faster, twisting, twisted. Twigs slap me, bark scrapes me, and thorns rip me as I fall. A thousand tiny indignities compound my injuries. I slam into a thick branch, crunching my ribs. They crack with a sickening sound. But that is not the end. My fall is broken but I am not at rest. I drop the last ten feet, landing like a dead-weight into the blanket of leaves and moss.

I am almost blinded by numerous excruciating agonies. I feel blood in my mouth. I see something white flecked with red, jutting jagged through my trouser leg. Smashed leaves and tree detritus fall down around me. Feathers flutter to earth with ethereal lightness. They use gravity as *their* plaything, coming to rest only when they wish.

Times passes. I don't know how long.

I open one eye. I see a face surrounded by light. I wonder if I have awoken, reborn again, somewhere else. But a paroxysm of pain tells me I am still in this world. The face belongs to The Boy in the Blue Coat Who Waved. He is sitting on his bicycle, one foot on the grass.

"I saw you fall. Just now," he says.

"I have… been falling… for a long time," I reply. The words come slowly, rasping and raw.

"Are you hurt?"

"I… am… broken."

The boy nods, as if taking this all in. "Are you are an angel?" he asks. "Only I've never seen one with such a big wonky nose before."

Richard Webb is a UK-based writer of long and short form SFF with stories published in British Fantasy Society magazine, Teleport magazine and several anthologies. He reviews SFF novels and is active on Twitter: @RaW_writing.

Thought Surgery won the British Fantasy Society 2020 Short Story Competition. We're happy to reprint it here.

The Coffee Shop Crowd
J. L. Royce

Jada walked in, assailed by the welcome smell of espresso, eager to get to work.

The net is a beast, always hungry, never satisfied…

Most people were head down with their gear, crouched in rows at the lines of smallish tables. Jada searched and found an empty spot—a *premium* corner. Hustling over, she claimed the chair with her draped jacket (*not* her bag) and stepped over to the counter.

Jada ordered her requisite skinny latte, waving her mobile at the register: the price of admission to this informal office. There was a backlog of orders from the busy drive-through. As she waited, Jada's eyes wandered the room, noticing some familiar faces. She wondered how many of the surrounding screens contained half-written blog posts and other piece work.

Or (Jada reminded herself) *unwritten* and *over*due—like her own.

First order of business: *topic*. Jada accepted her drink with thanks to the barista and made her way back to her coat, considering the problem. She was disappointed to find someone infringing on her space.

He'd sat down on the *very next* chair when he could have simply left a spot. Jada eased past him into the corner as he opened a convertible and fumbled out earbuds.

"'Scuse me," she mumbled. He blinked at her as she sat on her coat and laid out her bag.

She settled down, glancing over: *No drink.*

"They don't like it if you don't buy anything." Immediately she regretted the remark, sounding so *priggish.*

He grinned. "Put yours down between us, huh? They won't know who to kick out."

It wasn't an unpleasant smile, but not a particularly promising one, either. He turned back to his screen. The ensuing silence hung between them like bad breath on a date.

Resigned to her task, Jada's eyes casually moved from seat to seat: open screens, buds in place, and (the lucky few) charging cables filling power outlets. She prepared to follow the ritual, assume the position, but the familiarity of it all brought her up short.

What were they all *doing?* Jada counted eight—no, ten—sets of eyes on screens. She paused, the screen of her convertible half-raised.

Topic.

Careful not to make any obvious movement, Jada cast her eyes upon the intruder next to her. What was *he* doing? His screen was angled slightly towards her: there was a video playing, a street scene. Not a document, or a spreadsheet, or even an email: nothing useful. The news? Even porn would give her a better lead-in.

Jada yawned, stretched: always a good conversation starter, with guys.

"Well, I guess I should start working," she suggested. "What about you? Just waiting for someone?"

He ignored her, concentrating on his screen. Jada observed that there were several still pictures—people—displayed, along with a UI and text. The phone lying next to him purred, startling her. Its owner sat up, hitting Pause on the screen.

"Yes!"

Pulling the buds out of his ears, he tossed them on the table, picked up his phone, and stood. Almost as an afterthought, he looked at her.

"Did you say something?"

"Nothing important. Just wondered what you were working on."

"Oh…well, I just earned a premium drink—" he waved the phone excitedly "—so there's that. I'm gonna go order."

He grinned again. "Wouldn't want to get tossed out."

Without answering her question, he stepped around her (choosing to place his crotch, rather than his ass, in her face) and made for the register.

"Yeah—I'll explain in a minute."

As he happily engaged the barista, Jada took the opportunity to examine his screen more closely.

The video was paused: amateur-looking, handheld, a street scene—perhaps a protest, or a riot. The three faces displayed were all Middle Eastern males, dark-haired, with similar features. A timer was counting down—expiration?—and she pondered a footer that told her little: *PROJECT ASTREA – User: Chas – Owner: private.*

Alerted by a movement in her periphery, Jada glanced over as its owner stepped up for his drink. She quickly opened her screen and frowned in concentration at the authoring portal of her customer's site.

"Getting a lot done?" He sipped a tall iced drink, waiting for her to move so he could slide by. Jada transferred her cup from between their screens and scissored her legs together so he could pass.

"Not really. You?"

He waved the drink, then set it down. "Well, I'm a writer, but I was just doing some piecework…in between projects. Turking for the man…"

He settled in, adjusting the tilt of the screen.

"Yeah?" She prompted.

"Pays, a little." He turned the screen towards her. "Here."

"You watch a video and look for the faces shown. Simple, right? Except, you have to listen to word lists while you watch, and try to remember them."

"Sounds hard…Chas."

His eyes widened with a glimmer of uncertainty—fear?—until she pointed at his cup, where the barista's label was blurring from condensation.

"See?"

A look of relief softened his face. "Yeah, that's me."

"My name's Jada." She held up her beverage as if to validate her claim.

Chas laughed. "Kind of eerie, isn't it? Our cups know who we are."

"So does the barista, and her register, and the store app… Do you write fiction?"

His shrug was answer enough. "Want to see this? I have to restart anyway before the time runs out, or I lose points."

Chas touched the Reset icon, the screen blanked, and new choices were displayed. He put in his earbuds.

"Just follow along, this time." Jada nodded, and Chas hit Start.

The video was a protest, a street scene of chaos, smoke, and running people. Jada glanced at the faces, and back to the video.

"It's some sort of AI training—facial feature analysis, maybe? As soon as you recognize a face, you *tap* it—" Chas touched the second face in the list "—and keep going." He was speaking a little too loud, but no one seemed to notice.

Jada kept glancing back and forth, as the video panned the milling crowd. It wasn't at all easy, with the jittery camera, the smoke, and the squirming auto-focus.

Another face replaced the target. Jada blinked, staring.

"I think I recognize that one." She tapped Chas on the shoulder for his attention and repeated her observation.

"Doesn't matter," he muttered. "Just whether it's in the scene."

Uniforms—police, or soldiers—surged into the frame, wielding batons and using their shields to push back the civilians. Jada noticed the familiar face, holding a stone which he hurled at the helmeted head of an officer. She pointed.

"I'm *sure* I know him."

"Nice catch! You may have a talent." He poked the face, scoring a point.

Jada slipped out her phone, and leaning over, snapped a picture of the portrait on the screen.

"Hey! You're not supposed to record the work." Chas frowned at her, then returned to his task.

Jada passed the picture to a search engine. A moment later, the result was back.

She interrupted Chas again. "This doesn't make sense."

With an irritated glance, he pulled out a bud.

Jada waved her phone in front of him. "There—he's an Egyptian peace activist."

"So?"

"Look at these stories. He's not the rock-throwing type. And that scene was in Damascus, not Egypt. Where do they get these videos?"

Chas shook his head. "What does it matter? I got the points, didn't I?" He finished the task and paused the application.

"You don't have a problem with this, do you? Training AI? Worried about the Singularity?"

Jada smirked. "Of course not. AI is just marketing sizzle for the cloud platforms."

"Huh." He considered her. "Want to try?"

"Sure, I guess." Jada pulled her chair a little closer. "If it's not against the *rules*…"

Chas offered her the bud he had just removed. Jada took it, somewhat reluctantly.

"No ear infection."

Research. The topic was starting to gel.

She smiled back and inserted it (*still warm: shudder*).

"Ready?"

Jada nodded, and Chas once again reset and started.

The next video revealed a street at night, from overhead. The monochrome glare of night vision mode suggested a surveillance camera. A pair of figures drifted along, laughing and chatting.

The audio was unrelated: a woman's voice, reading a list of words: place names, interspersed with obscure English words.

Jada struggled to concentrate on them. *Vocabulary improvement.*

Chas was muttering in frustration. "I can't tell…"

The video blinked. The perspective shifted to a hotel lobby, well lit, another fixed camera looking down from high on a wall. Massive revolving doors rotated slowly, disgorging the laughing couple.

"Bingo." Chas poked the woman in the scene.

The murmuring in Jada's ear suddenly caught her attention.

…perihelion…cunnilingus…sententious… great fucks…broken…paraphilia…

She pulled the bud from her ear.

"And… got you." Chas touched a man in the video.

Jada waited until the screen blanked; but when she spoke, Chas shushed her with a wave.

"Wait, we still have to do the word lists."

A text box popped up, and he began reading, tapping the words he recognized.

"Yeah—well, that's the project, anyway. I can get bonus points if I sign you up." He stretched, noticed her. "Are you okay?"

"I thought you said it was place names," Jada objected. "Where are the rest of the words I heard?"

"What other words?"

Jada licked her lips. "Like— *cunnilingus?*"

He peered at the screen, pointing. "How about…*Cuyahoga?*"

"*Great fucks?*"

"*Grand Forks?*"

They continued back and forth, Jada's frustration growing until she threw up her hands.

Chas tried to placate her. "It isn't easy…maybe you just weren't listening closely enough."

"Or maybe the words were *different* in the left and right buds!"

Chas had a puzzled expression. "Why would they do that?"

"I dunno. It's *your* gig."

His screen blinked. Yet another video opened, paused. It showed a hotel room, empty, a king-sized bed visible: three pillows wide.

Chas looked at her. "Want to try another one?"

She pointed at the small objects dotting the pillows. "What's that…chocolates? Hey, I think I recognize this place."

The factory-produced art, the bold color patterns of the wallpaper on several surfaces, all looked familiar to Jada.

"All hotel rooms look the same; some are just more *same* than others."

Chas's finger hovered over the Start button. "Well?"

"What the hell…" Jada picked up the earbud, considered it, but returned it to Chas. "No audio, thanks anyway."

Her companion grinned and started the next test.

A timestamp burned into the image indicated it was early evening, some months back. Waiting for the action to begin, Jada wondered what she'd been doing that night.

"That was the weekend I went to Toledo for a wedding!"

Chas gave an irritated wave. The couple from the previous video came into view, entering the room. He helped her out of her overcoat, and removing his own, tossed them onto a side chair.

"I shared a room like this with a bridesmaid," Jada whispered. "She complained about being booked into a room with only one bed. Turns out she hooked up with some guy at the reception and didn't show up again until the next morning…"

Whether Chas heard her was unclear. The couple undressing each other had fixated him. Fresh faces were cycling on the side of the screen, and Chas scored the man. The woman, facing away from the camera, hadn't shown up yet.

The target pictures switched again—and Jada was looking at a photo of herself.

"Hey!" Chas glanced over at Jada, did a comical double-take, and returned his attention to the screen. "Why are *you* posted here? And we already identified the woman—"

The connecting door to an adjacent room was ajar. It swung open, and a third figure appeared, shadowed. She was dressed— barely—in lace and hosiery. The couple beckoned to her.

Chas' finger hovered over the targets— including Jada—offered on the screen.

The woman in the video stepped out of the doorway. "That's *not* me!" Jada hissed.

The figure passed through the cone of light cast by a hanging fixture: Jada.

"It can't be me!"

Chas, staring at the scene, paid no attention to her. He moved his finger over Jada's smiling face on the screen. With his other hand, he absently picked up his beverage and sipped it.

"That's not my…body—and I never dress like that, okay?"

Abruptly, he straightened in his chair and snapped the screen closed.

"Fine. I'll take your word for it. But if it's not you, how did you end up in the video?"

"Well, it's a fake—a well-done fake." Jada nodded to herself. "Certainly body-fakes are a thing."

"Are you a celebrity?" His tone was doubtful. "These fakes still take a lot of work. And what are the chances that somebody would make a video featuring you, and it becomes part of the project— when you're *not*—and it just happens to appear when you come in…"

Chas trailed off. Jada followed his gaze as it wandered the room. Several people staring at her looked away when noticed. A few more pointed phones in their direction.

Jada jumped out of her chair, nearly spilling her coffee, and rushed over to the nearest observer. She flipped the woman's screen around.

"Hey! I was just—"

It was the Astrea site, but a different video: a protest on a New York street, Jada throwing a bag of blood, striking a well-dressed woman.

Jada turned to the next member of the crowd: another screen, another video—a party scene. The target faces changed, and Jada was looking at her picture again.

"Play it!" Jada demanded. The woman touched Start.

It was a dimly lit handheld video: moving through a party, through a hall, to an open bedroom door. Inside, a cluster of drunken revelers surrounded a bed where a woman lay, legs spread, a man kneeling between them. When the woman lowered the liquor bottle she had been drinking from, Jada realized it was her face, leering at the camera.

She stumbled away, to another screen: a home security feed, Jada removing packages from a doorstep and running away.

There was a touch on her arm: Chas. Jada flinched.

"Come on, come back to the table." He looked pained.

Numb, Jada followed him. Chas urged her to sit down with him and bent close.

"I *swear*, I didn't realize it would recruit you—I've heard it hardly ever does, and never has from me." His voice was a pleading whisper. "You have to believe me…"

Chas picked up his screen. "I can fix this. I'll send you the access code—" Her convertible chimed, and she turned it over.

Welcome to Project Astrea, Jada! Terms and Conditions of Use:…

"Why would I do this?" Jada demanded. "Help it create a world of lies?"

"It will leave you alone if you just *help* it, watch videos, of other people…"

Jada scrolled. Her personal information populated automatically. Around her, more people were staring, raising phones, taking pictures. She scrolled faster—address, phone, email; driver's license, Social Security number, bank accounts, insurance policies; transcripts, publications, social media accounts; medical history, vaccination records, prescriptions, elective surgeries…

She touched the Accept icon.

The video disappeared from Chas' screen. Around the room, the crowd returned to their screens, once again ignoring Jada.

"It'll be all right, you'll see."

Chas looked at her with hollow eyes. "Just help the Project, put in your hours, collect your points, and it will leave you alone."

"It will all be fine…"

J. L. Royce is a published author of science fiction, the macabre, and whatever else strikes him. He lives in the northern reaches of the American Midwest. His work appears in Allegory, Ghostlight, Love Letters to Poe, *Mysterion,* parABnormal, Sci Phi, Utopia, Wyldblood, *etc. He is a member of HWA and GLAHW and was a Finalist in the Q3 2020 Writers of the Future competition. Some of his anthologized stories may be found at:* amazon.com/author/jlroyce.

Catch *his other story for us, No One Goes Lonely, in* Wyldblood #2

Wyldblood Magazine #6 available for pre-order!

If you like what you're reading and want to see more you can sign up to the next issue for delivery direct to your door or inbox.

£5.99/$7.99 print or £2.99/$3.99 digital.

www.wyldblood.com/magazine

Watch

Film and TV

This time around we're going to take a quick look at the new Netflix movie Boss Level, check in with the latest episodes of the Walking Dead and the Handmaid's Tale and reflect on Marvel's two big recent releases: Black Widow and Shang-Chi: The Legend of the Twelve Rings.

Boss Level first. This is a very slick and stylish action thriller with a solid Groundhog Day with (very big) guns vibe. It stars Frank Grillo as a man forced to relive a day in which a bizarre collection of bad guys try to kill him using swords, guns, helicopters, trucks and explosives. There's an estranged wife, a kid he doesn't see enough of (who's now in great danger), a suitably sinister turn from Mel Gibson and the end of the world, repeated daily. This could have gone horribly wrong but somehow it all comes together in a surprisingly satisfying way. Originally scheduled for cinema release back in 2019 it's been repeatedly delayed and now you can find it on Hulu in the States and Amazon Prime everywhere else.

The Walking Dead's back, for its final season (albeit one with 24 episodes, probably spread over a couple of years). We're a few episodes in at the time of writing and the action's hotting up in traditional fashion. The filming's been Covid-friendly, which presumably means more social distancing, though it's hard to tell from the finished product. Does it cover new ground? No. But that doesn't mean it's not as compelling as ever. This series has lost many viewers along the way as it's departed from the comic book source and some have felt dissatisfied with the plot's twists and turns (and some of the unfortunate deaths). And, of course, the former central character Rick Grimes (andrew Lincoln) is no longer with the show (though he's meant to be starring in a trio of much delayed spin-off films). This time around Alexandra, Hilltop and the other settlements are rebuilding after the struggles against last season's antagonists the Whisperers, and food is scarce leading the cast to embark on ever more dangerous forays into Walker-land to get supplies. Then new bad guys in fright masks start killing people, and series veteran Maggie must trust the infamous Negan if she – and her friends – are to survive.

It's still watchable, but there's a danger of overkill. There have already been a couple of spin-offs, with more in the pipeline and ratings *are* dropping (though still healthy).

But, ironically, given the zombie count, the Walking Dead is a survivor and it should flourish in its new home on Disney+.

The Handmaid's Tale (Hulu, Sky Atlantic) has also shown a longevity exceeding its two source books. Now in its fourth season, the embattled June is still trying to find her way clear of the oppressive Gilead, where women have no rights and are primarily viewed as breeding machines, suppressed by a brutally misogynist interpretation of scripture. Last time around, June helped a planeload of children escape to Canada, together with some of her handmaid friends. Can she get to Canada too? Expect some high profile series-regular deaths in this series. There's more to come (a fifth series has been confirmed) but Season 4's ten episodes of betrayal, cruelty, revenge, sacrifice and determination are more than enough to keep us going.

Finally, Marvel's two big summer releases: the long delayed Black Widow and the much anticipated Shang Chi: the Legend of the Ten Rings. Black Widow is Scarlett Johansson's payoff film for all those interminable supporting turns she's done over the last decade or so second stringing for Captain America and Iron Man.

Unfortunately, the payoff has become somewhat muted due to Covid 19 getting us to all stay at home and watch on Disney+'s premier subscription service (or not at all) so she's having to sue Disney for her promised millions. But bad blood behind the scenes aside, is the film any good? Yes it is, despite it being a prequel of sorts, set between Captain America: Civil War and Avengers: Infinity War. Natasha Romanov (Johansson) is a fugitive, hiding out in Norway, when she gets caught up in a scheme to free her former Russian colleagues, who like her were designated Black Widows. And to do so, she has to face off with classic Avengers villain the Taskmaster. It's a slick action movie squarely in the Marvel tradition and leaves you wanting more (which is a shame given the subsequent fate of the character and Johannson's plummeting relationship with the studio).

Shang-Chi and the Legend of the Ten Rings is an entirely different movie, though, and carries the Marvel movies in an intriguing new direction. Based on the successful 1970's comic book, Master

of Kung-Fu, the film is set in San Fransisco and follows a young martial arts expert (Shang Chi, played by Simu Liu) as he faces off against the Iron Gang, who killed his mother, and his father, the discoverer of the mystic and powerful 'ten rings': Wenwu. It's a fast paced action film which, like Black Panther, has a reach that extends well beyond Marvel's normal US-centric heroes. And it fits squarely in the Marvel Cinematic Universe, feeding directly into the upcoming Doctor Strange movie. And unlike Black Widow, this one's exclusively in cinemas for a short time. If anything can drag you back into the multiplex, maybe this is the film to do it. (MB)

Books

The Saints of Salvation
Peter F Hamilton

Peter F Hamilton is one of those writers who just can't do short – he's famous for multi-volume mammoth epics such as the *Night's Dawn* trilogy (where the dead come back to life (and not in a zombie way) and start to take over the galaxy), the *Commonwealth Saga* (where aggressive aliens are trapped in a Dyson Sphere for a reason – and we let them out) and the *Void Trilogy* (where there's a vast area of space which is subject to its own space and time rules – and it's expanding). So the three volume *Salvation Sequence* is exactly what we've come to expect from Hamilton – long, complex, hard SF with multiple plotlines, a large cast of characters, a fast moving narrative and plenty of action and suspense.

I should caveat this review by saying I don't understand much of the science, and I think I probably read whole chunks of this with the words just flowing pleasantly round my consciousness, a bit like (I imagine) all the carefully crafted sentences I aim at my dog do when he drools enthusiastically waiting for his treat. But that probably helps. When I think I *do* understand – for instance at one stage a neutron star is forced through a wormhole – I get pulled from the narrative trying to work out how it could possibly work. And how to visualise the binary star (where only one star is visible) that it's supposed to be colliding with. Cool idea, though.

Anyhow. The basic setup: Earth has been taken over by the alien Olyix, who are on a galaxy spanning mission to reach the God at the End of Time, and are scooping up any alien race they can find (including us) to joining them on their pilgrimage. Not voluntarily, of course, but 'cocooned' ready for whatever bonkers end of days revelation will come, and held in orbit round a gas giant where time has been slowed down (so the end comes, in relative terms, much faster.

The Saints of Salvation is the third and last book in the sequence. It's comparatively light for Hamilton at 511 pages but it certainly packs plenty in there. It covers twin time periods thousands of years apart linked by the 'Saints': five people who engineer the fightback against the Olyix in the 223rd Century and who follow their giant 'arkship', the *Salvation of Life* back to its base, 20,000 light years distant. They intend to send a signal when they get there, warning the rest of the galaxy. But with time flying so slowly round the Olyix base, there's always a chance they might be around when (and if) rescue arrives, many millennia later.

We're longstanding admirers of Peter F Hamilton and this book (and series) is a welcome addition to his work. It's been a while between volumes, though, so these books are no doubt best enjoyed read sequentially. It took me ages to remember